RIGIL

A RECOLLECTION THROUGH HIM

A Novel By

BUDD HANSEN

COPYRIGHT © 2021, 2024
ALL RIGHTS RESERVED | BUDD 'TK' HANSEN | Originally Published in the United States on *September 6, 2021*
VehicleDigest Publishing, LLC

RIGIL

A RECOLLECTION THROUGH HIM
www.BuddHansen.com
@VehicleDigest.net

WriteMe@BuddHansen.com

ISBN: 978-1-7332172-0-0 (Paperback)
ISBN: 978-1-7332172-1-7 (e-book)

COVER ART INSPIRATION: MARK OBRISKI
COVER ART DESIGN: TERRELL J.P.K.
EDITED: TERRELL J.P.K.

RIGIL

BUDD HANSEN

Journal Zero

She drop-kicks the glass doors of the lamp shop, and her wooden soles shatter it open. Her palms catch her fall, but not enough to protect her from broken glass scattered across the sidewalk. The mob tramples her through the entrance, running over her hands and face as glass cuts through the fabrics of her fingerless gloves and mask. Her skin is pierced, and she bleeds excessively onto the garments of others who she grabs in an attempt to stand. Blood drips across the concrete only to await a washing from the falling raindrops of the approaching nimbus clouds. Streetlights fall short of her light of glory as she reaches and screams, rolling toward the dive bar next door—where she's left curdled against the glass entry front in hopes they leave this place at peace.

...regardless, however, I should definitely call the police.

Four bomber-wearing hair-greasers leave the barber shop with combovers while the bakery two doors down is ransacked for their donuts of the week. One of the bomber-wearing guys in a blue romper hands a young boy a baton to swing at the revolving doors of the locksmith on Grant Street—but the baton bounces off the metal handle and nicks the boy across his bottom lip. He swings again in frustration, drops the baton, and kicks the door while the baton rolls beneath his feet. The boy slips on the baton, falling heels up, and slams the back of his head against the sidewalk. Blood drips from the corner of his lip, seeping between the crevices of the concrete sidewalk, and pours into the streets.

Someone has to have called the police by now…

A woman lifts the manhole at the intersection of 66th and Roman. Three of her best friends climb out carrying flag poles, gas cans, and water bottles. They wrap the end of the pole by the garment of the flag, light it, and wave the enflamed end, chanting:

> *"Hallelujah, here we stand,*
> *Hallelujah, we demand,*
> *We are tired of your payments,*
> *Exhausted working lay-folk,*
> *Hallelujah, hear our plea,*
> *My gosh, we hate to plead,*
> *Hallelujah, we demand,*

8

> *...end these payments,*
> *end this scam..."*

After six rounds of chanting, they pause for a water break. I sip my lemon-infused tea, pondering, stirring, lurking from above at a skilled mob attacking the storefronts of TheDistrict's most tangible assets. The steam from my tea joins the smoke of the flag, ascending 33 levels to the heights of Tower 521, where I stand, sipping my lemon-infused tea, watching it all steam. They begin chanting again, but this time in harmony and unison:

> *"Hallelujah, here we stand,*
> *Hallelujah, we demand,*
> *"Hallelujah, here we stand,*
> *Hallelujah, we demand..."*

A small group migrates closer to our intersection at Knolls Boulevard. The man whose leading, pumps his fist while pointing toward the apartment complex on Grant Street. The group follows him as they pass the coffee shop to approach the complex entrance. They're met by an older woman kneeling, praying, and pleading on her knees as she bows against the paved concrete of the parking lot's driveway. The leader slowly reaches to the woman's forehead—rubs it—then laughs, looking back at a few others who laugh with him, projecting the utmost humiliation of the woman praying on her knees.

...I'm sure her neighbors are calling the police at this point.

A girl in a grey sweatshirt, loose-fitted jeans, and lumber-soled boots sprints at full stride toward the group. "Straight ahead," she shouts. "Straight ahead," pointing directly toward the intersection of 66th and Knolls. The girl continues running while wrapping her palms with a red gauze. They march down 66th toward Knolls with the torched flags, signaling their remaining faction on Roman Street to join them. The groups come together in front of the untouchable coffee shop in such chaotic fashion—merging forces like the hundreds of people walking to cross all intersections through a pedestrian scramble. I lose sight of the woman as smoke from the torches cloud my view. Specs of them come in and out of sight as they approach closer and closer to Knolls. Further behind, Roman Street is left for dread—shattered glass across sidewalks, trashcans emptied, storefronts raided with products left in the streets, and cars vandalized, leaving their alarms in a panicking noise.

Red and blue lights tickle my peripheral as a convoy drives across 49th Street. The mob, however, paints our intersection of 66th and Knolls with the blood of the girl and out the lips of the boy. They stomp in unison, chanting their passionate desires and chucking enflamed flags at the entrance of our glass pivot doors. Tower 521's fire alarm sounds off as

I hear pounding at my door. I grab my phone and run through my apartment's corridor to answer. Chad frantically rushes shoulder first through my doorway, fingering through his hair. He storms to my corner wrapping window and stares miserably in disbelief—panting, huffing, and gasping, leaving strands of hair across the floor that'll soon join the dust balls beneath my couch. "Did you get my text?" he asks. "…you see what's going on?"

"Yeah, sorry," I respond. "I was just on the phone with the police."

JOURNAL I
TUESDAY—DAY ZERO

STIFF... AND TUMBLING THROUGH LIGHT. As above, so below, barreling through space. With gravity's permission, they drift until docking after an eternity of moments in flight. Unknown to their voyage's destination, dust particles are fascinating by how each ends up in a cluster beneath my bed. I would clean up down there, but what would the monster eat?

Nope... not me.

A text illuminates my L.D.S. screen, indicating Deliah has arrived with her crew. I sneeze downward through my apartment's corridor and notice five dust balls breezing across the open living room rugs.

What bothers?

My nose is runny.

There's a dirty shirt to blow in and a dirty shirt to collect the dust-ball party on my living room floor. Dirty shirts also wipe down tabletops and my fiberglass bookshelf holding 108 books, all of which to insist upon myself.

But this is ridiculous.

I should be in the elevator.

I massage my fingers with the moisturizing hand sanitizer Perkins mounted on the service elevator wall for movers. It doesn't quite glisten my knuckles before stopping at our lobby because so much of my skin yearns for water, that it screams itself to white.

"Say it ain't so…" says Perkins as I exit the elevator. He strides upright off our courtyard's pathway and through our lobby walkway wearing the custom sole Oxfords Chad gifted him last fall. He calculates each of his steps to cover the embroidered borders of our beige carpet—because it's me, who does the same, but only when I feel no other eyes are watching. His loosely fitted gray linen Capris stop high enough for his polyester dandelion socks to luster with his Oxford buckles. I can only imagine his CPAP machine has him sleeping better by how high his shirt is snapped just below his Adam's apple. "He would have never," Perkins whispers, shuffling a stack of papers on his concierge desk. He ganders at the courtyard and lowers his lenses.

"She passed the review test," I respond.

"She? How many stars?"

"Enough to be here."

"Her company, how many stars?"

"Their worst reviews had nothing to do with their work."

Again, he asks, "How many stars?"

"3.9, but—"

"As I said, he would have never."

…but there she stands with her two men—a caramel-complected queen gardener with perfect teeth, satin hair, and walnut brown eyes. I introduce myself to Santos, who wears the same gray oversized work shirt as Guala. They both grin—nodding and probing while slouching through their footsteps.

"Watch your step," I warn them as we approach the courtyard's pathway.

But Deliah, she doesn't.

Her shoe is caught against an old cinder block we never replaced—so she trips, stumbles, and kicks up old dusty rocks like an off-roading tire. I continue walking the micro-pebbled path bordered by bruised and broken-down cinder blocks. Deliah gathers her balance, puts her shoe back on, and catches up with my steps to where we walk in sync, crunching rocks down the walkway, toe to toe, and at a pace even the birds wouldn't have noticed who'd begun.

While speaking about a daphne and tulip garden at the center of our courtyard, I direct her attention to where residents and guests first go after walking a rather vapid path. We cross the fountain and approach the table where she lays out the sheet of their blueprint proposal, covering our limestone-finished tabletop. "That's it?" I ask. "Wow. It's Perfect. It's amazing." Deliah squints her left eye, shading her face. I can't tell if she's picking up my… or she loves her work. "The SUN should shine in, just like your smile."

She turns away, wiping her palms against the pockets of her cargo shorts. And I… swipe my fingers through the sitting waters of our matching Relic Nebbia fountains.

Though she gasps, it's subtle.

My guts do the same in a candid response—withholding a wonder of where that stupid comment takes me. Maybe a bit too early for the remark. But people like me, we just say shit.

◆

Because of its diagonal positioning and having been constructed between a grid of avenues, placed obscurely amongst several transversing streets, Tower 521 was destined to break code through development. The building stands at the end of a three-way intersection, where Knolls Boulevard and 66th Street cross the junction of 67th and Grant. The original proposal was presented to the firm that recruited me and five others out of two prominent Port Avantian universities. We were given pencils to mark nodes suggesting block location, spatial height for airspace, and the grounds to determine whether a parkade could be dug four levels deep. TheDistrict committees overseeing contract approvals and code regulations were tied up with recovery efforts from the riots out of Saint Laurent'co Circle—the communal square where our Bourgeoisie (Borj-Wah-Zee) Tower stands.

During construction, neighbors had no idea what was being erected on this obscure block. From the first week the site was fenced to excavators, backhoe loaders, telehandlers, and dump trucks moving on and off the site, it took the placement of two ridiculous cranes until the neighborhood started a petition against our new development.

Although Tower 521 is the only building with a view of the Bourgeoisie east of Laurent'co Circle, it's a viewpoint that's been investigated by the Chambers of Commerce since our first inspection was done. They found that the six-hundred-foot, 37-level residential tower wasn't built with protocol in mind. The morning International Building Code sent an emergency vehicle to test the lower-level entry of the parkade, we were cited for following through on level 13's floor plan.

Considering that our three open-air levels make it easy for the wind to gently say "Hi" and not shout "Hey" through swaying walls, Tower 521 was designed only to provide a strong Wi-Fi connection. Drive north toward another

Uptown, where they permit the construction of buildings higher than three stories, apartment complexes miss out on viewing the *fuck you* I placed where the old Laurent'co 'W' could be seen from miles away. Also, when standing three blocks from the front entrance on 66th and Grant Street, our 15-foot glass pivot doors give clear visibility through our lobby and out to the dual water fountains that center the courtyard.

But the escalating developments from a second riot out of Laurent'co Circle, is why the Tower's focal point, our courtyard, has been closed off for renovations.

1.2

THURSDAY—DAY ONE

Day one for Deliah's crew is two days after my awkward comment—and having to overcome the anxiety of thinking she'd report me to her commission.

…the way she digs on her knees, tossing dirt, creating dust clouds canvasing her half-cut short-sleeve top. The way her plaid rain boots catch her well-toned calves rubbed by a strip of tulip seeds hanging from her cargo shorts. It's also the way Guala and Santos wear loose hanging hoodies and matching mountain creek work boots that maybe the comment was inevitable—so I'll accept it. Because if I don't, my brain will circle the regret like a merry-go-round until I regurgitate my inner known lands of sea bark and citric molasses.

Guala waves over Deliah, and she stops digging to join the two in a huddling discussion. And through their mother tongue, Guala and Santos converse while Deliah stands, waiting, seemingly eager to become their ground's general. Guala repeatedly points toward the storage shed as Deliah steps through our lobby's south-end entrance, leaving dried mud clumps across the plastic film covering the beige carpet. She drags her feet across the covering, shifting the plastic lining and making imprints of her smothered foot tracks. Deliah looks down at her feet, scorned, and, "Oops," she says. "We'll clean that. Just trying to remove sand from out the pits. These fountains will have to be off for a while."

"Well…" I respond. "The breaker in the storage is connected to the lights for the service elevator."

"Do you guys have a backup generator?"

"Yeah, but we have maintenance people out for a few days."

"Hopefully, no one's moving in soon."

"But Perkins schedules me before my runs."

"To use the service elevator?" she asks. "Doesn't look like you're going for a run now."

"And?"

"I saw you come off—"

"I know."

"So you ride it every day?"

"And when I'm scheduled to."

"Okay, just asking," she says. "It's good you're staying active. I did gymnastics myself."

"Is that right? Then you should know of Dumbo?"

"Sure," she says. "Big ears?"

"Yep."

"Okay..."

"And he can fly, too."

"I'm aware."

"And then he's made fun of?"

"Sounds familiar."

"And his mom was captured?"

Deliah ponders, "I don't know the story that well."

"Oh, well, that's what I thought of when you mentioned gymnastics."

"I don't see the connection."

"Connection?" I ask. "Don't gymnasts do stuff with elephants?"

"Yeah, but do I look like I belong in a circus?"

"No, but certain gymnasts do stuff with elephants at the circus."

"Okay," she laughs. "But we were talking about your service elevator and running. You brought up an elephant."

"Where'd I lose you?"

"An elephant," she says.

"You mean Dumbo?"

"Yeah, sure."

"Okay, just making sure we're on the same page."

"I doubt we are."

"So, I did lose you?"

"When you brought up Dumbo, yes."

"I was also thinking about the main elevators I'll have to take for a week."

Deliah begs, "You're losing me…"

"With an elephant or gymnast?"

"Where's the connection between dumbo and your elevator?"

"Why does there need to be a connection?"

"Isn't that how conversations work?" she asks.

"You would think."

"So maybe you should."

"Should?"

"Think…"

"I should think? That's pretty normal."

She laughs, "Sorry, this conversation couldn't be any more random."

"For who?"

"For me."

"How so?"

"Dumbo," she says.

"I told you what came to mind."

"But what about this elephant and riding the main elevator is so…"

"So… what?"

"Inconvenient?"

"Well, for Dumbo, he didn't have tusks either."

"Tusks?"

"Yes," I respond. "Tusks."

"Now we're talking about tusks?"

"Yep. Tusks. We keep ours in that tool shed. Be sure it's locked up when you guys are done, so there's less stress on my part, okay?"

◆

Security is the space I prepare to reunite with the man who taught me preparation. He convinced Gus, my *father*, to journey with him from Ilorin to Nigeria's TrenchPort Valleys. And decades later, back to the United States District of the Atlantic Coast Shorelines.

Tuesday night, he phoned me from his hotel room to let me know he'd figured out how to fly back into Port Avanti International Airport. As a kiln builder turned hydropower technician, I could only wish that our reunion at the Locust Point Uptown is as revitalizing as TheDistrict's initiative to restore high rises across the historical settling pier.

Passing Swann Park and avoiding the McHenry Tunnel, unlike the first time, my dashboard illuminates brighter to ensure I exit right toward the National Monument at the Parkway. I pull up to Beets of Uptown and keep my eyes open for Nwaka, who I haven't seen in ten years.

I presume his face has filled out.

Often speaking his words in bodily gestures, I can never picture him still—he moves a lot. I imagine him, a walking hologram, by how his arms and legs shift, leaving a 3D drawing of his spoken words. His dramatic vibes create his solitude amongst any crowd. And his bushy chest hairs crawling out of his polo shirt—a badge of fraternal wisdom. He'd often stop and stare before speaking from the bottom of his breath. Then stop again, inhaling to check if he's understood.

…but Gus never mentioned him being anywhere on the spectrum.

Before I can scan my L.D.S. screen across the valet's drop-off station, Nwaka approaches from the lounge's revolving doors, praising, "Boy, you're tall," and holding his receding West African tongue. He attracts nearby calculating eyes while grabbing me by each of my biceps and wrapping his arms around my shoulders. "I still remember you, a boy," he says, pushing me away at arm's length to examine me from head to toe.

"And still, tall, dark, and handsome."

We enter the bar, and I glance through the Beets' main waiting area, where their lo-fi indie music absorbs space between bar-basking Avantians, hinting at a mellow scene for the evening. Vodka-mixed aromas excite Nwaka through a low-lit atmosphere, but scanning deeper reveals many more scattered silhouettes of sitting shadows. We approach the bar, settling near the bussing station, and I request my first water. "I no get, my boy," says Nwaka. "Avoiding the serpent's juice? I'm here for you."

"And here I am."

"You stressed?"

"Just dealing with losses."

"Losses? You playing ball again?" he asks.

"No. Our tower because it's just me."

"What happened?"

"Somebody woke up."

"From sleep?"

"No. From bed."

"So they never fell asleep?"

"No," I respond. "They never got out of bed."

"*They* weren't ready? But who—"

"The dummies…"

"Give up the ghost, sheesh," Nwaka begs. "Looters aren't the same people who get it."

"So, you understand who woke up?"

Nwaka shakes his head in disgust. "You own that building down in Capitol Parish?"

"Not entirely. I have the constituents."

"Who?" he asks.

"Them…"

"I'm listening," says Nwaka.

"And so are they."

"Seriously?" he whispers. "At least you're finding ways to beat those housing the Joneses."

"I never met the Joneses."

"But we prepared you for them," he winks. "You're glowing."

"Like the colors above Laurent'co Circle, right? They're a mess… Still beautiful, though—."

"Though what? And colors? You're talking that *weird* shit again."

"No I'm not."

"Yeah, you are. And look at you," he says, shoving my shoulder. "Looking like a left-behind dry seed. I brought lotion from my room if you need it."

I spread my fingers above the bar's SpacePad screen, shedding light across my skin. He's right. So I take his tube of lotion. As the bartender grabs ice to mix my first drink, she watches me moisturize in this very building, formerly a family-owned funeral home. Above her psychedelic-funk halter top are mismatched earrings, stretching both canals and aiding her ear-hustle. It also helps that her hair is pulled back, tri-colored lipstick glows, and cleavage is exposed, that we attract drunken breaths. And as many other candor eyes brush by, honing for our smile, resting beast-face doesn't eye back. Nwaka, however, a lush in his element.

"But seriously," says Nwaka. "Who are they?"

"Who?"

He tilts his head and rolls his eyes. "I need names, not ghosts."

I take a glance at the people around the bar and respond, "*Their* ears aren't painted."

"C'mon," Nwaka begs, doing another bar probe. "You're nothing like Gus. It must be this District water." He grabs my cup and gargles a mouthful of my ice water.

"Speaking of?" I ask. "You flew alone."

"She won't do a long haul with me."

"I knew of one who did."

Nwaka glances up toward the Eurofase looking chandelier, licking his lips. "Oh my, her?" he says. "You're really bringing her up after all these years?"

The question... it bothers—a question not even the

depths of a social medium can answer. But I've asked, and something must be done about the elephant I've pulled out of my back pocket that sits, sips, and shares this tainted Avantian tap water with me. Fortunately, we finish it before heading into a stall to log one and lotion up.

Returning to the bar, I inhale deeply in preparation for the extra three shadows gathered around Nwaka—including a short older man dangling his feet from the bar stool I sat at.

1.4

"This is the boy, Ahli," Nwaka points, grabbing my forearm. He introduces an older sandal-wearing man, an earthy-driven girl, and a boy standing beside them who could be any age my junior. But age is one of the few spectrums that fool me. "I was telling them about Dronya, Bhavana, and Pranantika—our TrenchPort Valleys," Nwaka praises. "I wish we had the time so I could tell them all about it."

The bartender raises her eyebrows, rinsing a cup for ice, and asks, "You still have family living there?"

"Family?" Nwaka ponders. "You're looking at the *light of our last*. But I'm here on holiday. From Iceland. This boy here, nothing less than a son of mine."

The younger girl shows us her L.D.S. screen, "This is

TrenchPort," she says, displaying a postcard-looking scene with muddy air masking the pollution. The brightened screenshot saturates the clouds above our Panaya's ripples and flushed for a serene aquatic attraction.

But that's not true.

She points to the tallest casino, standing 700 feet tall and 70 yards from the riverfront shores. And between its sister resorts are rows of beach volleyball courts next to beige sunbathing chairs reclined for the bourgeois to sit. The photo exaggerates an egg yolk SUN and a river so blue by the sands so bland beneath a SUN so faint.

"It hasn't always been this way," says the older man, still sitting in my seat, swinging his feet.

Nwaka points to the girl's screen, saying, "We left long before this here riverwalk. And from what I remember, they'd cleared this entire riverbank, including everything, for about a 300-mile radius."

"Sounds familiar," the older man says. "My great-great grandparents landed right here, Locust Point, off a boat from—"

"That's not the same," the girl interrupts.

"We all came here against some ill will," the older man tells the girl. "But, of course, you're too young to understand this."

Nwaka faces the bartender in a sidebar conversation,

pawning the three off to me.

"What was it like coming all this way?" the older man asks.

"We just left," I respond as his eyes glisten and flutter.

"You left? Like that?"

"Yes. Like that…"

"Okay," he responds.

I nudge Nwaka's shoulder, pleading, "Can you tell them?"

"What?" Nwaka flinches, turning to face the group.

"They're asking us the question."

"We flew the fuck out."

"Okay," says the man. "No one just flies out of their country."

"Oh yes we did and just like this…"

.
.

"Ahliko," shouts Nwaka. "Where are you going?" He slams his drink on the bar top and marches to the entrance, stopping me just outside the doorway. "Were you gonna say goodbye?"

"No. I just needed fresh air."

"Okay, well, the bartender's comping our drinks. Have a little."

"After a little fresh air, sure."

"Okay. But don't leave."

"I won't."

"I'm not here for long," he says. "Okay?"

"Okay."

"I came here for you."

"And I was prepared, but only for you."

Nwaka laughs so hard that he grazes my elbow, scraping the melanin off my wrinkling skin. "C'mon," he smiles. "Is that enough—"

"Dummies?"

"No."

"Then what?" I ask.

"Fresh air."

"Let me check…"

Nwaka crosses his arms. Leans against the building. But shakes his head in shame of the demon he witnesses suck in ounces of air no different than laundry powder is snorted by the boys who can't party past midnight but are also too young to call it a night at ten o'clock. "Ready now?" he asks.

"Not yet."

"Sheesh," he says. "I'll make sure you get your seat back."

"Some things aren't worth getting back."

["Abeg."]

My RyderCar drops me off at our Knolls Boulevard entrance. I take the main elevator to level 33 and keycard into my apartment's corridor. Temp-control powers on, making it comfortable enough to remove my plaid top and bottom jeans. I leap chest first onto my bed, roll to my back, and stare at my ceiling because it's that time of night when the monster revisits the day *ThePeople* punted our Robo vacuum through the lobby, relieved themselves all over the courtyard, and came back in to mix up the silverware in the restaurant we had to close.

My left leg bends inward so I can position my hill against the inner muscles of my right thigh. And beside each hip, my index and thumbs connect to spread the other three fingers while docking into Pier III. This resting position commences a venture through Mahan—my meditative voyage until sleep.

…but what usually floats behind my eyelids isn't so shifty tonight. And these phosphenes aren't so colorful. One glides across my blood vessels and doesn't move when I watch it. Its outer layer has a spiraling effect, altering black and white, spinning like the jet engines that propelled me into the Port Avanti International Airport. It's a similar floaty from what I watched through a flight of lucid dreams—creating The Mahan of Pier III—a space emerging from a cloudy red room, echoing *her* vocal white noise.

Yet still, I muse into sleep on the viewing dock of my meditative happy place—recollecting the years that brought me to a bed where a monster lurks below. Growing up in The Valleys of TrenchPort, this monster stood by me through each village we settled. It even helped me pack after Gus told us to.

◆

◆

◆

BHAVANA'S EXODUS

"Remi, Ahli," Gus shouts. "Come here, now." We follow the projection of Gus's voice, bouncing off our adobe-paved walls and through the openings of which you'd think a window should be. Remi shuffles her feet across the long rugs covering our dirt-wrapped floor. Gus waits outside our front entryway as we approach him beneath his stone-cold, settling face. He nods toward the wooden-carved bench, pacing beneath our tarp-covered patio hanging by its last three roped threads. "Listen," he says, contemplating. "I need you both to pack everything you'll need for three to four days."

"We're leaving?" Remi asks.

"Just pack a bag. It'll be a long flight."

"To where?" she asks. "Did Nwaka say where?" Grimacing in silence, Gus stares into the pastures, pointing beyond the meadows. "Why would he put us on an

Aeroplane?" Remi asks.

"Banks in TheValleys no longer honor our checks."

"And the bank you guys built?"

"Build anything around here—"

"...and *they* will come," she whispers.

JOURNAL II

BHAVANA'S EXODUS(CONT'D)

HOME ALONE ONE AFTERNOON, REMI'S near the back door, fucking around, doing her coloring book activities. Cattle bells across the pasture in Pranantika are silenced as our SUN reaches its peak. My morning's gracious bowl of oats burns off through my throat, thundering within my esophagus. But as our next meal awaits at another curve of the clock, we watch as *they* do, but never fear as they approach.

Walking up to our front patio, she strides her tall, dark Lady-Gal legs toward our door—wearing black and no green. With each arm swinging in front of her cargo-dressed hips, she catches my eye and steps closer to our doorway. I greet her, "Hi."

"Hello, young boy. Are your parents here?"

"No. Not here."

"Are you sure?" she asks.

"Yeah. Should I leave him a question from you?"

The lady doesn't respond, but she turns and walks away. She glances back, and her eyes belittle the very knowing of my stance. I picture Remi drawing a note to tell on me as the woman stops at the end of our patio and whistles while eyeing the homes of Bhavana. My tongue dances down the back of my throat to her harmonious lips and scathing eyes—a tell-all of what's next—as this home, too, has its passing.

.

.

.

Gus warned us to never approach the door unless Nwaka or one of their workers knocked. With unsecured entryways and neither of them ever home until dusk, we learn that what adults do with the resources they're granted is beyond the scope of a young boy's world and a precocious girl's mind. A week after the Lady-Gal's visit, Remi and I eavesdrop on the conversation between an exile and rogue hopeful. I take the rusted stool next to a soot-covered kiln, and Remi sits cris cross applesauce behind a stack of broken fire pit bricks. Birds cover our fidgeting legs, pushing sand and clay across our feet. Limbs from a tree we can never name drape across the side of our patio's opening, leaving us to watch as best a child could see. The community of Cicadas and katydids sing the white noise of our lands as we try listening as best a child can hear.

"…the hell am I supposed to do?" Gus whispers.

"Prepare Remi and prepare Ahli," Nwaka pleads. "I'll take the money. And then we take flight."

"Again, that money is for our people. You want us to tuck our tails and run like some timid dog?"

"Yusmata—"

"Why do you speak my name as such?"

"Because now you can hear me. Untuck the tail and listen. Can you trust me, your brother?"

"It's about our people trusting us," says Gus.

"But we don't own them."

"We own their land."

"And for how much longer?"

"Not for as long as they'll need us."

"Honestly, I think it's time we say…"

"Say what?"

"Fuck them," Nwaka whispers.

"Fuck who?"

"The people."

"Why the people?"

"Again, fuck all of them," Nwaka says louder.

"You're a filth."

"I'm okay with that."

"You disgust me."

"Want me to say it again?"

"You're selfish. Listen to you. People count on that voice."

"Not anymore," Nwaka smirks. "You must not hear me, fuck all of them."

"And leave them starved, deserted? You're foolish."

"Eiyaah," Nwaka praises. "The sound of freedom can be so pitiful, don't you agree?"

"And you call yourself a man of faith with a tongue so dry? You should be thanking GOD for those people."

Nwaka stomps the patio floorboard, shouting, "Fuck him too."

I turn to Remi, having never heard a fuck so aggressive. Yet, in a silent shuffle between them, dirt powders across their boots, both gifted from Avantian Big-Men.

"Or the French?"

But this silence… a tug of war between one fool stressing out of respect—and an ego, respectfully, stressed out.

"…throwing 'fucks' at everything until I fold," says Gus. "I'm not dancing to the shit coming off that tongue."

"We risk our lives every day to build for people who'd never do the same for us," Nwaka claims. "Who do you think GOD is?"

"Not this."

"Because he is law."

"And we've broken enough of it."

"But for who? They aren't collecting the boys for any other reason but to—"

"So what do you think we create for these people?"

"Love. Security, and—"

"Did you hear yourself a second ago?" Gus asks.

"I did."

Gus laughs, responding, "...gotta come better than that."

"You think it's funny?"

"I think you're a hypocrite."

"That's because you want to think GOD is on this land," Nwaka begs. He stands through a silent response from Gus, cracking the boards of our makeshift porch—pacing, breathing, and praying for an exile's liberation. "It's best we walk the deserted plains now or do so at their will. And guess who gets the money then?"

"I would never—"

"As long as you're alive, maybe so. But promise me, you'll at least prepare the kids," Nwaka pleads.

.

.

.

For decades, authorities investigated Gus and Nwaka's crew—from subordinates of local politicians, utility board members, and underpaid regime leaders—all manipulated into humane androids.

…being against TheValley's enforced policies, Gus and Nwaka become frogs boiling in hot water. Today, however, history fails to explain the frog jumping out before becoming white meat.

II.2

"They're spraying. Let's go," Gus urges, yanking covers off my back. Mounds of dusted dirt settled in the corner walls tremble to the sounds of a stampede, amplified as though the cattle are running under duress. I glance out the window, and the last calf scurries into the feather grass fields as its tail disappears through the meadows.

Haze across our common's drift from the smokey fields, carrying a familiar scent—signaling an exodus from the infernos of *them*.

I rush toward the front doorway and grab the backpack packed two days prior. Remi stands beside the bench, pointing at Nwaka, who's running from the backside of our house in a whispering shout, "I told you," he says, angered. "It didn't have to be like this. For us—."

"You think I care for an 'I told you so' right now?" Gus shouts, storming out the front door, leading with his finger.

"…watchers are leading everyone to the other side of the pastures," Nwaka whispers.

"Alright, let's go."

"No. It's time. This is done. They'll spray a little longer and wait it out."

"We'll die," Gus warns. "Flames will carry over from the crops."

"Just trust me. It's a decoy."

Gus waves, gesturing we follow. But two steps out, Nwaka grabs me and Remi by our forearms. "Let them go, you fool," Gus shouts.

Nwaka palms our foreheads, hushing Gus as he pushes us to kneel against the entryway. "They don't know where they're being led," Nwaka whispers.

"I saw a BlackSuit," Gus urges. "Let's go."

"You saw a suit? In the dark…" says Nwaka as he steps in front of him—but Gus turns his back.

Nwaka continues to pull our shirts over our noses. "They'll suffocate," says Gus.

Nwaka stands before us as Gus attempts to reach for our arms, but Nwaka smacks his hand and shouts, "This… should never be a fight, especially here."

Gus takes three long steps, throws his arms up, and locks his hands at the back of his head. He watches our people scurry off the land, one family at a time, carrying what they can and leaving what they want… amidst the heat radiating across the village from our burning feather grass fields being blackened across our settlement of despair. The sky, however, lit—brightened by our full Buck MOON still shining between our passage of trust.

And it's there... where Gus squints, lurking at Bhavana's entry gate at what emerges onto the entry trail. She runs toward us, crossing Bhavana's Garden and haloed by the brightest bulb of our midnight skies. "Nwaka," *she* cries.

◆

◆

◆

Per usual, but with her, we're off seeking between villages—scouring across Central Nigeria's abundant dry land. Along three SUN torched roads and twice on a musty bus, walking past one settlement to another with stacked corpses are no longer our checkpoints. Nor are carcasses lying roadside a reason to give up. But the last collection of bodies we see lined up face down, side by side, disintegrate as lappet-faced vultures flock up high, preparing to dive into their latest chew beneath blanched skin. Their bareheaded beaks first snatch the dangling intestines because there lay fewer bones to peck through, leaving their protein and nutrients to be served at VILLAGEROCK'S temperature. That's if they don't care to work for it... but for most of these remains, their organs have been protruding through skin since the heart had a beat.

No one fed them. We got lucky. And for every question we ask en route, the longer it takes to get there.

To where?

We often don't know.

And neither does she.

But unlike most, we lay soil upon many lands because we learned to shut up and keep walking, keep boarding, keep going, and stop talking. We're fortunate; however, this time is weird. We're heading to an airplane.

...just as we trekked the other expeditions, we get there, and Gus reminds us to never look back. But Mahan—created on this journey—presents memories by default when meditating into sleep.

My home, that void, comes first—as it arises between the colors floating behind my eyelids. These aren't just phosphenes or eye floaties, but space I must overcome every day. They're often presented as the people we've left behind. And as each particle fades in passing, I'd tell them, *"We're sorry. We couldn't save you all..."*

Where I'm raised, where I'm cultured, no man could write. But from the reformed Middle Belt and the failed Sharia Laws, we don't know our history. Instead, we were taught to understand ourselves.

How I'm protected?

How I'm of the fortunate few?

I don't know.

But I am… nothing else than a drift of dust on its eternal voyage.

…when *she* returned to the gates of the sistering villages of Pranantika and Bhavana to conclude her story, no woman could nurture upon the lands of my surviving remorse.

So why did she care?

What was her interest?

To see a boy dream?

Or watch a girl loathe?

So be it en route,

We fly, we leave.

♦

♦

♦

Our first wheels-down at P.A.X., it takes a while to deboard the plane. As the last to inhale 14 hours of recycled air and free meals, we walk by left-behind trash scattered next to unbuckled seatbelts, crumbs hanging from seat cushions, and cleaners rushing before the turnaround flight departs back across the pond. Exiting the jetway, we enter the gate to a crowd of Avantians lined up at our left and right—all waiting to greet the latest arriving international passengers. Slowly walking between them, Remi lifts her right arm and slices her hand through the air with wavering, flickering fingers.

"Monkey see, monkey do."

"They're waiting to board the next flight," says Gus, smacking down our swaying hands. He pulls Remi and I by our wrists, clearing us away from the walkway. I turn around, and a gray-haired lady waves back, smiling through her thick-framed black glasses.

Gus walks five steps ahead through the terminal walkway, making it difficult for me to stomp the lines between the black and white tiled floor. He checks our backside every ten seconds as though he's counting the rib-shaped wall panels between shops and restrooms. The same panels, but red and black, hang tall and free between each gate as the intercom echoes out of each triangular opening. But I'd say it's the circular signs extending from the bottom of each terminal signage that Gus could be ignoring.

We approach customs, and the officer asks, "Passport or immigration status, please?" Gus rummages through his bag and hands our documents through the glass receiver. The customs officer inspects our papers and scans them between two yellow lasered lights. "Mr. Slick, Jack Slick?" the officer confirms.

Gus responds, "Yes. Yes, sir." I watch Remi stare up at Gus, perplexed, lips crumpling and eyes gleaming.

She's confused.

"Mr. Slick, can you attest on behalf of these two?" the officer asks.

"Yes. Yes, sir," Gus responds.

The officer reads off a line of terms and stipulations. He then glances up, telling Gus, "Eye's here, please," and continues reading. After each sentence, he ensures Mr. Jack Slick is paying full attention. "Sign here," he says, pushing three forms through the glass receiver.

Gus grabs the forms, scribbles his name, and we leave.

We head to the departure's curbside platform and request a RyderCar at a standby station. Gus rubs the machines as though his curiosity alone will bring us a car.

"Need help with that?" an airport worker asks. But Gus waves him off.

When a car arrives, Gus sits up front while Remi and I ride in the backseat. We drive off, and three thumps against the quarter panel bumper rumbles my seat as someone shouts, "Mr. Slick, Mr. Slick." Gus groans and puts his head down when the window beside him automatically rolls down.

The gasping customs agent asks through the window, "I believe you signed your son's name? Yusmata?" he asks, showing Gus the erroneous signature.

"Yes. Yes, sir," says Gus. "Jet lag must be getting to me."

"But then what'll be my name?" Remi asks.

Gus raises his finger, but the agent interrupts, "This is Port Avanti," he winks. "You're free to make a name for yourself. Your father can tell you all about it."

…a place where sunray avoids concrete and lives coarsely shy of its citizens. The SUN tries in the spring, giving its most effort in the summer, but finds itself blocked by towering buildings, grouped corner by corner like a motherboard. This computer, however, collects tens of millions of breaths left behind by Avantians, forgetting to take a moment to breathe.

But imagine if they did? What else would we have seeping out sewage canals and between alleyways? Maybe a wasteful society who'll re-indulge their filth? Yet stay blind to this cycle of anxiety, and a channeling of ignorance screaming from a faction amongst them?

♦

…although this isn't what I saw leaving the airport, it's the same SUN shining since arriving to the TheDistrict— where we're first dropped off at the building where the 'W' was.

Gus is led to the entrance by the building's leaking Avon aromas. He gets in line and directs us to stand beside the double doors adjacent to a beam of sunlight reflecting off the marble-painted floors. It creates a visible SUN ray through both sides… where each Avantian, from business casual to formal wear, walks beside the heated light strip as though a beam of sunlight could impose their purpose.

"Excuse you, sir, don't you think we all are?" A woman's

stern voice echoes over the building's interior white noise. "Stand down," she demands. A brunette-topped male security guard stands at Gus's right arm. And the woman in a Vanta dress on his left shoulder wears a perm. The woman faces the guard, allowing Gus to step away and re-approach the teller.

Moving through the shadows of our SUN's glare, the woman's arms swing wide from left to right as her hands and fingers sway to her voice's command. I can't make out her words, but the security guard stands with his chest out and eyes at her attention. Gus then grabs an envelope from the teller and urges us to follow him out the door.

After crossing the street, Gus pulls Remi and I to the side to stand beneath a moving fixture of neon billboard lights. We watch him sidestep pedestrians as he rushes back across Broadway Street, waving down the lady from the bank. She stops and turns, looking Gus up and down as though he's lost his mind.

In their quick exchange, he returns, pocketing a piece of paper. "What's that?" Remi asks.

"It's for later," he responds. Gus snaps his fingers for Remi to grab my hand. "Hurry. We're meeting up with Nwaka."

Nearing the side of Gus's hip, Remi asks, "That lady was in black. Didn't you see?"

"She also wore a name badge," he chuckles. "Didn't you

see?"

Gus wipes his forehead with his t-shirt nineteen times during our 45-minute walk to the gray brick building with three arched entry fronts—Capitol Parish Union Station. We ride the escalating stairs underground for the GTube's SouthStation tracks, where a checkered departure platform and several waiting passengers stand below flickering LED lights for a train that'll eventually arrive and then depart. The air's cooler, but our ride isn't long enough to dry Gus's sweaty armpits and soaked shirt. However, long enough to study the professor at the charging station reading a book with a namesake collage as its cover. The lady next to him is writing—likely musing out the degenerate boy band near the staircase, planting numbers in the heads of impatiently waiting riders as they sing:

> *"Teachers on strike,*
> *no more school today...*
> *they want more money,*
> *but the board won't pay."*

First stop, the newly established lounge, Beets of SouthTown—where Nwaka and the Lady-Gal sit at a table for five. Each SpacePad above our gold-shaded table setting lights up as we grab our seats near the revolving belt of drinks. And just past the lone waitress serving the corner wrapping table at the window, an orchestrated happening of new developments, proceeding as so…

Several construction signs and yellow coned barriers surround a giant caterpillar loader full of gravel. A monstrous excavator dumps massive loads of broken-down street concrete beside an unfinished curb. A worker sidesteps a sinkhole as his fellow hard-hatted men yell at cars detouring the site. The block's sidewalks aren't done, and the next street over is closed. Whosoever ensures the flaggers signal appropriately is one bad verb from a tragic *oops*.

"Ahliko, is it Mahan? Is that a township back up north?" Nwaka asks, returning from the drink belt.

Gus responds, "No, not by us. He probably overheard from cattlemen."

"You sleep loud and crazy," says Nwaka.

"On the plane? What did I say?"

"Mostly mumble-jumble. But something about my hands, ma' hams, or ma' some—."

"The boy reads," says Gus.

"Which means he speaks," Nwaka responds.

But there's a frog in my throat—ribbiting at the moment awkward becomes my middle name. "I can't explain Mahan. Why do you care for?" I ask.

Remi plants her eager face above her crossed arms on

the tabletop. I lean back—and through my armrest, there's space to take in. So, I look there.

Remi also gazes through this empty space, making it the moment when a kid must explain his imaginary happy place around big sister.

But it, too, is under construction.

Meanwhile, Gus warns Nwaka, "Listen, just be careful where you show those papers. We got through customs alright, but the bank got suspicious."

"We won't be here long," says Nwaka. "Too much peopling going on around here, you see?" Nwaka points, sneering around the restaurant.

"Where would you go?"

"You mean we?" Nwaka clarifies. "They have public libraries. We can book a flight back out by Friday."

"And stay on the run? You afraid of someone?"

"I'm more afraid that everyone's afraid."

"You realize if it wasn't for the woman at the bank, we wouldn't be eating?"

"Good. Let's keep moving while our luck is high."

"She was black."

"Was she wearing black?"

"Black on black," says Gus.

"What kind of black?"

"C'mon…"

"Dead clocks strike on time twice a day," says Nwaka. "You beg for the two-year struggle guarantee, don't you?"

"No, but I'm also not addicted to struggling like the sum of us..."

"Please, brother, look at you. You can afford the Ryder."

"And?"

"Mr. Slick? Your sweaty palms and face tells it all."

"You would never understand if all you have to worry about is—"

"Go ahead. Say it," Nwaka dares. "And so *she* can hear you."

"All I'm saying, what good is keeping these two on the run with me?"

"Because we didn't take the money to spend it in this drudge-heavy city. You settle these kids here, and by high school, you'll be speaking to them from your grave."

"Why go there? Their ears aren't painted."

"...at least they'll hear where your body is shipped—"

Gus snatches his water and jerks the cup at Nwaka's face, splashing water across his chest.

Nwaka shivers,

...gasping for air.

His shirt...soaked.

The cup...empty.

Nwaka whispers, "If our Foola could see this."

"We were nothing, or ever like them," says Gus.

"No. Not Mr. Slick."

…and still, as does a portrait on the wall, *she* remains silent, staring and sitting pretty.

Chiming glasses drown out the frustration of simmering steaks steaming across our nostrils. It's not only the embarrassment amongst the people, but our food comes late. Beta trialing Server-Bots roll pass as Gus and Nwaka's energy diverts our readiness for our food's setting. Nwaka's voice attracts the curious smiles of nosey dining Avantians—all oblivious to how we've come off a dirt road, flying time machine, robotic taxi, and a train to understand one thing.

Everything we experience has its passing.

Because nothing lasts forever.

Except this one thing.

For me—at least.

II.4

Our first elevator ride takes us 21 floors up—where we rest across from Jack London Square Station's arching phosphorescent lights. Our beds lie adjacent to the station's glooming glow, seeping into our hotel room windows through the evening. Bedside binoculars give clear views across the Potomac and into Arlington—where some still question TheDistrict's incentives on keeping that city's name.

Watching Gus change his shirt and untie the blinds, our room dims but becomes ambient by the strike of a match. He lights the candles at the end of his nightstand and kneels at the shoulder of his bed. He gathers his hands on his lap and lifts his chin for the heavens to hear. Meanwhile, Remi and I tuck ourselves into the other queen bed to sleep head to toe.

We can assume Mr. Jack Slick prays. We can also assume he weeps by the sniffles above his sheets. But as Remi untucks herself, she crouches to sit bedside next to Gus, handing him tissues from the nightstand. "Dad, your eyes," she says. She rubs his back on his eighth sniffle, whispering in tune… a rhythm I'm unfamiliar with, but maybe a melody I've slept through—or a harmony we've lauded over the many men of protection and guidance:

"Daddy, oh daddy, please don't you cry,
The SUN still shines down on our story that thrives,
We'll need you on this land, as many have tried,
I'll wipe your tears for now, so please stop the cry.
Give thanks with me for a safe journey through night,
You're strong to follow your heart against a fight,
So hold your tears for now 'cause we'll be alright…"

We check out the following morning and walk six blocks to check in to another room.

Why?

We don't know.

But I presume it's Mr. Slick who exits the room for another visit to the bank, leaving Remi and I alone to soak up the awkwardness two siblings must address where one makes the other feel really stupid. "So, what's Mahan?" Remi asks, heading to the floor for her backpack. She pulls out her sketchbook and doodles her bullshit.

"You can't draw it if that's what you're wondering."

"But what is it?"

"For now, it's a desert of warped colors."

"What? Where?"

"Rub your eyes for a few seconds, then you'll see it."

"You're dumb. No one's going to do that."

"It's not for everyone."

"Then you better not go around talking about it."

"I don't."

"Then how did Nwaka hear about it?"

"I didn't tell him."

"But if you say it's a colorful desert, why can't I draw it?"

"...hard to explain."

"Why?"

"For the same reasons you're afraid of black."

"Shut up," she says, flicking her yellow-colored pencil at me. But I flinch, and it grazes my ear, landing on the AC vent.

"Remember reading *Untouchable* with the tech tint kids?" she asks.

"Yeah, Vinetra had us read it at camp last summer."

"*They're* going to think you're a walking Amaya."

"Who's they?"

"Good question. But thinking the way you do, you'll be alone forever, and no one will care to hear about your make-believe sleepy place," she says, giggling to the tune of her etching pencil.

"Whatever. I know what I see."

She laughs louder, whispering, "Delusional?"

"Remember how everything's been burnt? Dronya, sprayed. Puro Village, sprayed. Sambahula and Anatirikta, torched. And blow gardens, Vizala and Tola?"

Remi counts on her fingers, responding, "Forgetting three?"

"Yep, and even there, we don't ever go back."

"And we don't look back."

"But guess where I can always go back?"

"Nowhere after you're shot through your head. Get over yourself." Remi rests her head against the carpet between the beds and continues to draw, mumbling, "All you did was remind me of the places our Lady-Gals went missing, asshole."

I smother my face between two pillows to rid the echoes

of her sketching utensils. After five minutes, I peek over to watch her lion come to fruition and a forest of trees canvas distorted sunlight above the heat-emitting asphalt. By Mahan's rule, she's doing it. "What are you looking at?" she glares.

"I could burn that drawing, and you'd still be here crying, thinking those animals are becoming white meat."

Remi's chin elevates as she continues her menacing glare through the back of my skull. She pushes her bottom lip, tilts her head, and cracks her neck, preparing her words to hit like a Djembe. "You don't even know why you were in that group with those kids, do you?"

"We were in it together with Vinetra, and you left. You hated books and computer stuff."

"She also talked a lot. But I was in that group to watch you. I left because you ended up doing well."

"What's your point?"

"The camp advisers put you on the spectrum."

"We were special."

"Spectrum," she shouts.

"Spectrum?"

"Yes, spectrum." Remi continues coloring in the shades of her lion's tail, chuckling, murmuring, "Yeah...like why they thought Gavin couldn't find his way back to Bhavana. Weren't you helping out at the Panaya's outfall dump earlier that day?"

I grab the matches off the nightstand. Strike one with my

fingers. And toss it toward the end of our bed. It lands at the corner of Remi's sketchbook, and she jumps to her feet, screaming, "You idiot."

She tosses the enflamed sketchbook across the bed, and it lands on the floor, between the wall and dry comforter. I roll over as three-foot flames sprout toward the ceiling. The upsurging flares trigger the sprinklers, and the fire alarm sounds off. Remi fingers through her hair and rushes to the bathroom.

"Oops..."

The door is pounded three times.

JOURNAL III
FRIDAY—DAY TWO

FRIDAY MORNING, I ENTER A main elevator, and Perkins mentions two residents will get on at levels 19 and 13. I lean further in my corner, heel-deep in the checkered carpet, gazing into my bracing soul through the elevator's ceiling mirror.

Level 19 enters. A blonde man dressed in an industrial romper—reluctant at the eye, but he goes for it anyway, asking, "I assume we're going to the same place?"

"Down?" I respond. "Yes."

"I'm talking about work, brother. Gotta keep food in the fridge. Must be new to the tower?"

"Nope."

The elevator door opens for level 13. Her floral skirt stops at her calves. Pearl bracelet thick enough to be a beacon of contentment. She stands and stares, resting each hand against her love handles. "Donny," she says. "Well, how are you?" She gives Donny a punch on the shoulder for joy—and praises, "It's Friday…!"

"How else?" Donny responds. "On to where the SUN don't shine. How are your boys?"

"They're alive and well. My youngest is getting ready for college. So we'll be spending the rest of spring helping him prepare all his stuff," she says.

I insist they both exit first into the lobby walkway. It's the best I can do.

"Were you nice to our residents?" Perkins asks as I approach his desk. With his short-sleeved creased polo exposing the sharpest ends of his collar bones, he must be counting on SUN breaks coming through the lobby, much like the morning breeze is drafting along with residents and vendors coming and going from each entrance.

"Yep," I respond. "Donny was just telling me about his boys getting ready for college." Perkins leans over his concierge desk, and his geriatric glass-bottled fragrance leaks from the top of his unbuttoned polo.

"Donny's boys? Is that right?" he mumbles, typing on his SpacePad screen as his fragrance reeks over the desk's surface.

Deliah approaches with a blueprint layout of the garden. She lays it across the desk, and Perkins scans it onto our digital drive. "Is this what you laid out on Tuesday?" I ask Deliah.

"That was just a proposal," she says. "I couldn't tell if you actually wanted to go with that."

"What did I say about it?"

"Really?"

Perkins shakes his head, muttering, "Ridiculous."

But I savor the silence, soaking the moment, and think what next should a man say while his mindful manhole is uncovered. "...Perk, can you reschedule the appraisers?" I ask.

"Is the building going on sale?" Deliah asks.

"*They're* putting everything on sale," I respond. Deliah, however, finds it necessary to roll her eyes and walk away. But maybe it was me? Perhaps my tone? Possibly my body language. But I'd argue my eyes—considering today, Deliah's eyes are a faint copper-buffed coin. Her face flushed as the faux Buddha. Body stiff as the knave undertaker. Yet she loosens up, heading for the storage shed, where I notice a hoe and two shovels hanging out the doorway. "Why is the latch down on the storage?" I ask.

Perkins responds, "I must've left it unlocked after her guys cleaned up last night."

"You did?" I ask. "That's not good. You know who

would've never…"

…but Perkins doesn't like that.

So Perkins walks away…

He meets Deliah at the shed, where she's grabbing the two shovels hanging halfway out the door, leaving the hoe to fall all the way out. It lands across Perkins' Oxford shoes, but he only smiles and pats her back in forgiveness. Deliah tries kneeling to pick up the hoe but instead steps on the fiberglass end of the rake. The wooden handle flings up as she reaches to grab it, but her hand-eye coordination is nothing shy of a precocious toddler as it smacks her knee and then her nose. They both laugh in comedic fashion—but I don't find it funny—watching Perkins leave his key in the storage shed's lock-latch.

♦

♦

♦

The hoe in our storage could plow mounds of dirt out of Jala Village. Irrelevant today, but that village is where dust first rose as fire and smoke directed every moonlight's path. Hot enough to distort drunken faces through space—I never got close to the flames because kilns would kill when parents weren't watching their kids. They got burnt…and often…by dancing too close, carrying an internal joy. Or women sat resting their feet to release their day's catalyst.

Although we find this scene again attending the Capitol

Parish Church of GOD in CHRIST, there are no fires. Their communion trey serving almonds and beet juice as the body and blood of CHRIST, stays full. No one's baptized—but the treys circulate the congregation across navy blue pews like an ordained snack. From the English they shout, to the tones they praise, I never understood them—especially how they seek forgiveness for the same sin week after week.

At least that's what the pastor says.

…often spoken like a pastor, Gus taught us the best lesson about air and heat; 'never turn your back on either one.' As a wise survival tool, forget one, and you die.

But our hotel room burning wouldn't be the first time I'd learn that his lessons are like being nice to people.

…you have to remember to do that.

III.2

BHAVANA'S EXODUS (CONT'D)

The phone rings. They're pounding on our door. Remi swings at twelve-inch blazes of flames with wet towels as smoke smothers the headboard. I pull Gus's luggage from beneath the sprinklers as the door handle is tugged and jerked open. Three men crouch through the hall, extinguishing the bed as the wallpaper melts. They cover us in a foil-looking blanket and escort us into the hallway. I turn back to grab our bags and, "Leave it," the man shouts. "You kids okay? Any burns?" he asks, pushing us further down the hall. "Is it just the two of you?"

Remi catches a deep breath and gasps at my forehead. Thinking she'd be our spokeswoman, I instead leer down the carpeted hallway—because it's a long hallway— in fact, longer than the hall outside the room 21 floors up where we stayed last night. I could run it in one breath, but our bags are still in the room, soaked.

Facing down the hall, I sprint at the peak of my heartbeat, thumping with vigor. By the time Remi opens her mouth, I'm 33 heartbeats past the ice machine.

…no,

I stay put.

Running is the monster.

"Do either of you want to tell us what happened in there?" the maintenance man asks. The guy who extinguished the flames walks out of the room, slowly stepping down the hallway, holding burnt matches. "It's okay to be honest with us; no one is in trouble. We're just glad you kids are safe."

Remi clears her throat and glares at my collarbone. I veer my eyes left as they do it best alone—avoiding the trouble— avoiding her scorn. Remi, again, clears her throat and tells the man, "We messed up, okay?"

Room 927 is where they move us. It's a larger room with

a view of an 18-story tower across the street where they probably do computer chip stuff and outsource human resources to our kin over yonder. The room has a long, narrow entrance, but at least the ice machine is actually next to our sink. There's a refrigerator with a minibar, from juice bottles and yogurt packs, to spiritual drinks that'll trigger Gus's tab upon movement. The shower is stand-up only next to a green bathing tub—but I can't swim. We get two couches and an area with three desks. But without Remi's sketchbook, they're useless.

"Why are you just lying there?" Remi asks.

"I'm tired."

"You better be thinking about how you're going to explain this to Gus."

"It'll come to me in my sleep."

"But why would you do that?"

"You could've blew it out."

"Blew it out? Are you that dumb?" says Remi. "And you just stood there, watching. This could've been so much worse. When Gus finds out—."

"Maybe he won't."

"How? They have to stop him in the lobby before he comes up. But seriously, you're still doing it, just lying there."

"I didn't fall asleep last night."

"Why not? You sleep on an aeroplane but not on a real

bed?"

"I don't know, Remi. I guess so. But I'm tired."

"This isn't about you. What are you going to tell Gus?"

"…you could've blown out the matches."

"You set my book on fire, asshole."

"Well, you shouldn't have made me mad."

"What did I say?" she asks.

"You know what you said."

"About Gavin?"

"Stop it, Remi."

"Oh, that got you up? Thought you were tired?"

"I'll just tell him this was your fault."

"How?"

"You could've blew it out."

"Wow…You can't even think straight. What'd you do? Just watch the ceiling all night?"

"Yeah."

"You're ridiculous," she says. "I'm going downstairs to get paper."

I lie back down. But not for long. It's a trance-like sleep where I try ignoring my heart, punching through my chest. The best part, however, is the air conditioner blowing a fresh lavender scent across my covers. We're also high enough to where the chaos below is blocked by stormproof windows. But not by much:

People shout.

Cars honk.

Dogs bark.

…this is white noise.

Without birds.

Sometimes, I wonder if I slept or forgot to count my breaths. Sometimes, I ponder: if I didn't have a dream, was I sleeping? Or did I blink for a very, very long time?

◆

"One day here, and we're living like Phat-Cats," says Gus, hovering over Remi's shoulder. I lie on the couch, half awake, watching Gus, bright-eyed and boy-fooled joyful. "Did the sprinklers damage my bag? What are you drawing, my little lady?" he asks.

"No. Ahli moved most of our stuff before it got worse."

"Hopefully, these penthouse sprinklers know when there's an actual fire," says Gus. "And you would think they'd have this fire system tested before guest stay… a malfunction? Please."

"Malfunction?" Remi says.

"I mean, that's what the manager downstairs said…"

"That's interesting."

Gus rummages through his bags, setting baked chicken and salad wraps across the bar table. He then walks to his room, pulls out a pair of pants from his shopping bag, and lays them across the bed. He pairs them with three different colored shirts, laying out Velcro trap sneakers he pulled from another shopping tote. He sits, gazing toward me on the couch, but my eyes stay shut because to him, I'm definitely asleep. "Has he been sleeping like this since you two been up here?" Gus asks.

"Sleeping like what?"

"...lying stiff and rigid."

"He said he didn't sleep last night."

Gus chuckles, "Yeah. Right. Did he have a vigil through the night or something?"

"A vigil?"

"Like a night watcher, or—"

"Post Watcher?" Remi guesses.

"Something like that. But as stiff as he sleeps... Did he drink the embalming fluid downstairs?"

"He drank something that made him upset."

"How so?" Gus asks.

"I accidentally called him a name when you were gone.

"Did he hit you?"

"No."

"Speaking of names, you two might be starting school in a couple of weeks. I'll be out and about again tomorrow looking at a few."

"Okay, but will you at least tell the people my real

name?" Remi pleads.

On our first day at Saimre Joseph Prep, Gus sends us on our way from the Lone Avenue GTube station. Arriving at the blackened brick school building, having missed our first three classes, I'm put in the seventh grade, and Remi's good enough for the ninth. I eat alone for 25 minutes and later instructed to leave with this kid screeching the polished cafeteria floors with the bottoms of his rubber soles. He does this all the way to the blacktop, never looking me in the eye or asking if I appreciate his behavior.

I'm immediately approached by three curly-haired girls, one brunette, and a boy, asking, "Rigil, are you Rigil? My friend thinks you're hot!"

"What?" I ask. "Why do you say my name like this?"

The kid, who I presume is the group's leader, responds, "You don't talk like you're not from here."

They each gaze, mesmerized by my corduroy blue and white collar that's halfway popped. The brunette steps closer, covering her mouth. "Oh my gosh," she says, "Can I feel your hair?"

And I let her.

Annoyed for not knowing which girl says I'm cute, I accept their invite anyway to play a hopping-in-the-box-like game. The boy instructs me by pointing toward my feet as I step and hop. "You're not doing it right," he says, grabbing my arm. "You have to hop two times, step into this square, and then jump with one foot to finish inside the lines."

"Okay. I'll try again."

"Back in line and wait your turn—again." With his finger in which I wish to snap, he points it past five kids to the end of the line.

The last kid standing in line, the floor screecher, eagerly waiting his turn, looks to my neckline and asks, "Do you play basketball?"

"I've never touched one."

"Why not? They have extra balls—and then we can play."

The kid looks onward to the blacktop courts, jumping back and forth—maybe indecisive about hopping or shooting. So, I ask, "Do you know how to play?"

"Yeah. Me and my dad watch the boys play the other schools, and they try to win. They're the tall boys." He then points, looking down at his buckled shoes, and shuffles his feet as he did in the cafeteria, making skid marks on the concrete in a spinning motion.

"I think we lost him..."

But that's okay; many more groups of kids who aren't old enough for off-campus lunch are scattered around the blacktop—like the basketball court, where I'm recruited by the eyes of my kin as though I belong. "Hey, we need one more," the boy says, tossing the ball at my chest. I'm a half-second late to collapse my hands around the ball so it drops, bouncing off the Velcro strap of my left shoe.

I pick it up as two kids chuckle, "Hell no!"

So, I throw it back, shouting, "I don't play."

"C'mon, just guard him," he begs, rolling the ball back at my feet. "Shoot for who checks up first."

But I tell them, "I gotta use the bathroom." Underhanding the ball back onto the court, one kid picks it up, holding it with my wet palm signature impressed on it.

Eventually, the bell rings, and all the students walk toward the doors in a mass exodus off the blacktop. I contemplate holding the door for a couple of kids—it's the best I can do—but I'm pushed aside by a staff member who props the door open against a grounded magnet. He positions himself inside the entrance, standing in a dusty corner, monitoring students entering the school's barest hallway.

The halls are color-coded by classroom subject: green and brown for applied sciences, orange and blue for environmental sciences, beige and brown for cultural studies, white for math, purple for English, and the language hall is a collage of flags from every country. There's a black and red checker-walled hallway, but I'll only tour the east halls as long as I keep my hands and feet to myself.

My sixth-period class is on the beige side of the hall—a social studies classroom with rows of metal desk chairs, two digital clocks, and a magnetic carbon chalkboard up front. The teacher enters, asking, "And you must be?"

"My name?"

"You're Remilee's younger brother, aren't you?"

"Yes. She's my sister. I'm Ahliko."

"Rigil," she says.

"Does the paper say how you spell it?"

"I did the class a favor and wrote it on our announcement board," she points, giggling. "But it's great to meet you, Rigil. I'm Mrs. Schmidt. Today's lesson should be exciting."

You would think the school was having an emergency by how kids get louder through the halls, slamming locker doors and stomping their shoes against the floors polished by janitors every night after eight o'clock. Seven of these kids enter the classroom one after another, and Mrs. Schmidt quiets them because she knows the worst has yet to enter.

The last kid walks in with his hat backwards, pointing directly through me and snickering with the others. "Awe, guys, look, we get sloth hands," he says.

Mrs. Schmidt warns him, "Tokaiya, not today."

One girl stares—at me, palming her bottom lip. Her two

friends do the same because they're probably dummies who can't think for themselves.

But I can.

That's why I stare between my knees.

Then Mrs. Schmidt approaches my desk, again, kneeling to ask, "The other class had your sister get up to introduce herself. Would you mind?"

"No."

"Great. Just tell everyone your name, where you're from, and how—."

"I meant no; I don't want to."

"Why not? You'll feel welcomed."

"Just go away, okay?"

"Alright," she says. "I know a shy eye when I see one."

Mrs. Schmidt announces my presence to the class. As I raise my hand, three kids spit an earful of chuckles, *"At you,"* says the monster, *"You're the joke."* And so, I can't help but dream up each of their colluding corpses lying atop our most recent passings out of Bhavana…

.
.
.

I pull out my ViDi notepad, drawing trees, boats, airplanes, and landmarks we passed en route to me— becoming this artistic elephant in a classroom. I gaze into the tiled floor texture, redesigning it through mindless sketching as my eyelids weigh heavy and thinking what next to draw.

I'm sleepy.

I keep to my breath until stepping selfishly from my desk and into the aisle to head toward the door. I turn the handle and, "Rigil," says Mrs. Schmidt. "Hallways are closed ten minutes before and after each bell."

"But the door's unlocked."

"Do you need a restroom break? I haven't dismissed you."

"But I used it before lunch."

"So, where are you going?" she asks.

"I'm going to be right back."

I get a better look at the lawn next to the concrete blacktop, which I missed through all the chaos during recess. It's much greener than the lawn at the church Gus took us to until getting what he needed from the congregation—because church covered us until some logistics company in West Uptown hired him to commence his 18-month countdown to LEIP checks.

At least that's what he says.

And from there on, much like a church, the Meriwether Island trail loop takes his Sunday mornings, where I tag along to watch pickup basketball at the Ravana Park courts. I hear

Gus singing through his strides, inhaling aggressively through his nose and profusely out his mouth. He sings so loud that some of the ballplayers get too distracted to play—explaining why it's one of the few courts they'll ever play on.

III.4

It's October's first Thursday, and an urge to dribble burns at the palms of my right hand. My longing to feel what I last dropped out of fear and angst, worries my very assumptions of whether or not the game will love me back. My eagerness builds through the morning because I know that come lunchtime, I can do something about my sweaty palms dripping between the cracks of Ms. Hopper's classroom floor. And fortunately, by the time I get to Mrs. Schmidt's, I'll be rested with enough serotonin and endorphins to have circulated Mahan's vessel.

I skip lunch to be first out to the courts, check out a basketball, and experience it bounce right back but into my left palm. Cluelessly dribbling toward the court, the ball goes off my knee, foot, and anywhere it can find its way further away from me. It rolls into the teacher's parking lot three times while attempting to drive against imaginary opponents.

Seven minutes later, "Yo, kid, let's run twos." It's Tokaiya calling me over. "Hurry over before the others come out." On my way over, I rub both hands dry on the sides of my sweatpants' pockets. "Thought you'd run away again like a scared cat," he says.

Immediately, the boys position themselves, but away from me. I assumingly stand between the lower block, just beneath the net. Tokaiya grabs me by my turtleneck, pulling me to the top of the three-point line to face the kid passing in the ball. "Checkup," the boy says, tossing the ball at my gut.

Tokaiya shouts, "What are you… Pay attention. Hands up!"

The boy, our opponent, underhands the ball to his teammate, runs behind me to the hoop, and gets it back at the basket to effortlessly lay it in—concluding my first experience against the 'give and go.'

"Losers. Ball up," says Tokaiya.

Tokaiya stands above the three-point line and points to the corner. "Get away from him," he says. I sprint to the other side of the court, catch the ball just inside the three-point line, and "…shoot it," Tokaiya shouts. But I pause. I look. And two collapsing arms rush toward me as I chuck the ball at the rim.

The boy rolls his fists, calling, "Travel. That's steps, bro, c'mon…"

Tokaiya shakes his head and sprints toward the parking lot before my airball bounces and rolls beneath a parked car. He trots back, bear-hugging the ball as though it's his one and only true love—because it likely is. "You see this," he says, holding the ball at my nose. "Have you seen the game of basketball? Have you ever watched this ball go into the net?" But a car alarm sounds off, and so, that's where I walk. Tokiaya exhales aggressively out his nose, yelling, "Where are you going?"

"What's wrong with the car?" I ask. "Did I break it?"

The boy and his teammate—our opponent—stand restlessly as Tokaiya kneels in frustration and disbelief. "If you want to play, act like it," says Tokaiya.

.

.

Tokaiya scores our winning basket and immediately sits beneath the net, gassed, breathing heavily over the basketball. Looking at the older kids picking for five on five, he shakes his head, asking, "So, you do know how to play?"

"I mean, it's what they did."

"Yeah, but we ain't getting away with that over there."

"Is that where we play next?" I ask, pointing to the older kids. "Are they our next level?"

Again, Tokaiya shakes his head and walks away. "Bro...the fuck are you talking about?" he mumbles.

Bewildering in thought across the blacktop, passing cliques of kids on phones, hopscotch kids hopping, kickballs being kicked, and soccer—nothing more appeals—than to look back to a hoop and a ball as it's all I'd given a go. Yet in this autumn moment of realization, a tear out of my lonesome lures through my bottom left eyelash—and the left one, only. I stop to kneel against the corner brick wall, praying for the bell to ring because it should at any given breath of mine. But since I skipped lunch, I can skip making friends. And who of these kids would care? Who would accept me? Who's of my kin to skin anyway? More concerning, however, I just don't care. I honestly don't care. As though I should…

Suppose we—the kids of my kin—are put up against these black brick walls. I'd be that one black brick causing a cosmetic eye sore like the rare black car that's aggressively priced on the dealership lot because people can't tell if it's black or the darkest navy blue they can mix. People then wonder if it belongs next to the other blacks…

People look twice.

People question it.

Is it the type of black where, under sunlight, it looks different, reflects oddly, and tans slowly?

So be it; not everyone who looks like me is like me—nor views the world like me. No one taught me this; it's just how I feel—so…

♦
♦
♦

Since we're enrolled at the tail end of Joe' Prep's staff

and teacher-led strike, the union granted permission to contract counselors who could do so much more between regional school districts. Standing five feet ten inches, Dr. Carson Brody takes the office with two ferns beside the door. They just gave her the office for students like myself. So, the office is not hers year-round. I hear the last counselor left during the strike to become an astrophysicist.

At least that's what Tokaiya says.

Our first meeting is later than expected. It's well into the year and after the many moments when I've daydreamed myself out of class and into the ether of space where teachers are more than concerned about my ability to understand the curriculum.

"Rigil?" Dr. Brody asks. "I heard your father call you Ahli; which do you prefer?" Her smile invites me into her teeth—a perfected row of incisors enclosed between straightened canines. Also, porcelain polished, bringing out the true depths of her mid-aging dimples. "I'm the school counselor," she says. "You can also talk to Mr. Maurice. I believe you met him through Coach McCall?"

"I don't know either of them."

"…thought I heard you were conditioning with the basketball team," she ponders. "Gosh, it must be a Monday. Anyways, how are you adjusting to all this? Our rowdy kids, the city streets, buses, and trains? Sounds like your father found employment?"

"It's been mostly what I expected."

"Okay. And are you and your sister doing well at home?"

"What's wrong with her?"

"Well, at least you seem to be disengaged in most of your classes. And I know this can all be challenging. Are you not interested?"

"In what?"

"It's important that you take everything in," Dr. Brody says. "You can't expect to always get by on your looks. You could be expecting LEIP as early as your sophomore year. Will you be turning 16 by then?"

"I think so."

"So there, you're well on your way in less than three years. But we must first figure out what moves you, got it?"

"We just walk a lot."

"No. I mean, what excites you? What motivates you or inspires you?"

"What I see out of?"

"Explain."

"Naw, you wouldn't get it..."

"Okay..." she ponders. "I know you and your sister enjoy drawing?"

"Yeah, like CAD? We used to work on Yanaka back in summer camps."

"I see. And sounds like you were taught our English pretty well. But math—you'll need math, especially with CAD."

"We learned a lot of that stuff on the go. They taught us the basics."

Dr. Brody clinches her bottom jaw, cautiously squinting her eyes as though we could never have been so well informed. "Can you explain that, please?" she asks.

"Math, astrology, history, and geography."

"The missionaries did? I remember your father telling me about your summer camps near the townships you grew up in."

"But math was just the patterns we learned on the side."

"On the side? Math trains the brain for critical abstract thinking," she says, rolling her eyes. And then it's a long eye flicker as she asks, "You do understand that, correct?" Instead of answering, I admire her tri-colored earrings—the colors are more than just a rainbow, dangling and brazing her broad shoulders. "Rigil, can you at least tell me what inspired or motivated you back home?"

"A lot of places were called home. And for the regimes, too. Like in Vizala and Jala. But the last place is where we had to change our tongue. Or else they'd know we were exiles."

"Yes, your family moved a lot."

"Everybody did. Especially after witnessing the process."

"Process?" she asks, as her eyes stutter and lips pull closer.

Air passes my unbrushed tongue, trickling down the back of my throat as I respond, "Clean up." Dr. Brody drops her pen as I continue, "Since they'd line up all the—."

"Okay," she says, showing me the '*M*'s across her palms. "Just so you understand, our meeting is to gauge your ability to comprehend English and ensure your emotional levels are well and stable. It's been a few months, and teachers are only concerned because you sit quite reserved."

"I've been sitting in my assigned seat."

"Again, it's Monday," she smirks. "…and we all need a day to readjust into the week. We'll keep in touch every Monday or Tuesday. Can I surprise you with a call into one of your classes, and you can come to my office? Which class bores you the most?"

"Mrs. Schmidt's classroom. But she also lets me leave around my 108th breath."

Dr. Brody scribbles an aggressive note on her notepad. Two weeks later, I'm prescribed an extracurricular.

III.5

HIGH SCHOOL DAZE

Mid-summer, going into my freshman year, McCall gets the varsity head coach job at Saimre Joseph Prep, where he holds recommended conditioning practice all summer, starting at dawn four days a week. The monster I journey with sits while Coach McCall shouts, "Cones, Banks, cones! Run baseline and pivot those flat ass feet... And don't you dare touch a fuckin' ball til' that chest burns."

...watching me condition through a heavy chest, shortened breath, and my inaugural muscle cramps, we don't ever yell back—and it's not that I would. There are just certain things you don't say aloud to adults because when players do or overreact, McCall makes them run to touch every pivotal line on the basketball court—warning them when they're done, "It's only one step from teammate to hallmate," concluding a drill once named after having the intent of *self-natural* selection.

Before the first day of school, I'm one of 49 freshmen running the courts for 13 roster spots on their frosh-squad, three for junior varsity, and one to none for varsity. McCall approaches me as we end our last conditioning session of the summer. "Banks," he shouts. "My office." I squeeze by unpacked boxes stacked against each doorway wall. McCall repeatedly clicks his pen, pacing beside the office lockers. He sits in his tall black chair behind his N-shaped desk, observing each bare wall in ponderance and spraying the two fake plants beside his desk. He's not tall, but he says so by how he speaks from his intercostal space—the air between his ribs. It surprises me how far the game of basketball has taken his bulldog-shaped figure. He's fat but arguably thick-boned. His presence is commanding, with calves as thick as his thighs and forearms having more girth than an elephant's front legs. "Listen, Banks," he says, clicking his pen faster—and clicking his pen harder. "Do you know you sucked at basketball? I didn't like you. Maurice and I prayed you'd quit by July. Do you understand your odds, boy?"

"Odds? No."

"Why not?"

"Because you decide who plays."

"Yes, we do. But you're assuming there's another boy better than you."

"Okay."

McCall turns away, confused and baffled at my response. He kicks his feet up, resting his chubby legs on the ottoman, asking, "Ever been out to the Ravana Courts?"

"Yeah, with Gus while he runs."

"Gosh, I knew I'd love that motherfucker."

"Why?"

"You know, he told me we can't always win by getting a hold of our better selves."

"What's that mean?"

"It means go speak to your father."

"I can't if he's sleeping."

McCall exhales, shakes his head, and grabs a spray bottle.

"You see these two faux plants?" he asks. "I spray them with this here rose water to keep dust off."

"Okay."

"Don't wait until the grass is greener."

"What's that mean?"

"Again, go and speak to your father."

"When he's sleeping?"

"Banks, I've got a kid who'll walk through that door in about three minutes. So far, he hasn't asked me any questions."

♦
♦
♦

The following weekend, I meet McCall five levels beneath SouthStation: the junction for all GTube trains departing south of Capitol Parish. We arrive at Ravana Park courts with an overcast approaching and a cool enough breeze to dry my palms. The lawn is green enough to sit on, next to a row of freshwater fountains for the rich joggers to drink from at some point during their pointless runs.

Before McCall and his boys tip-off, he calls me over to center court. "Boys, this is Banks," says McCall. "Who's here to watch."

They each tower over my head, looking down through my Velcro straps and green sweatpants—nodding without a smile as if I'm here to steal their lunch. One of them asks,

"Can the boy speak?"

And another guy mumbles. "Can this one actually play?"

"Watch it," says McCall. "You mad because grades did all your playing? …Banks, I've coached these boys since grade school, from rec ball to JV at Lieberman High."

I shake their hands, introducing them by my name and not the awkward one, which a couple of them actually get. But Gus never told me how to enunciate it, so I really don't care.

"…you boys will see Banks running his generation out of every District Gymnasium," McCall preaches. "I can't afford his fragile legs to get hurt, especially after working those pancaked feet all summer. The boy showed up on time every day and still stunk it up in rec ball for two years. He wasn't good."

One guy laughs, stuttering, "That's it?"

McCall chucks the ball at his belly as the guy beside him turns his face. "You fuckers still listening for reactions?" says McCall. "No wonder these courts are as far as you've gotten."

Two guys hold in their laugh as one responds, "Damn. I get it, coach. Much respect. Especially if he'll be doing it in those," the guy says, pointing at my sneakers. Two guys turn away in an open-mouth burst of laughter. But it doesn't dawn on me until after my walk back to the mid-court bench when I exhale and watch them go at it, what exactly they were laughing at.

McCall's first to rush at every towering kid who's 20 years his junior. While manning their zone defense, his pestering pale hands agitates one of the tall boys, who laughed at my shoes. "Fuck!" he shouts.

McCall's steal gives him an open breakaway layup. On the next play, one guy dunks, rattling the rim back and forth. A smooth exchange onto the other end leads McCall for a collapsing drive and dish to his teammate, who launches a contested long bomb five dribbles behind the three-point arc. While admiring McCall's laser beam passes burn skin off each teammate's hand, the game progresses swiftly, giving me the eagerness for what I could envision tonight in bed.

McCall's top-of-the-key elbow jumper swishes through the net. "Ball game, suckas," he chants, slamming the ball onto the court. He shakes his head at the empty mid-court bench and turns in a 360 until he finds me on the park bench beneath an oak tree. He points, asking, "Why are you over there?"

"The SUN got hot."

"It's barely out. Did you see my shot?"

"Yeah, I can see past the tree."

He tilts his head, giving me his wicked eye. "I brought you here to watch, and you had them laughing at you, again, asleep."

"I wasn't sleeping."

"Oh, of course, daydreaming? Like in class?" he asks.

"No. In class, I'm sleeping."

"You looking to end up like those boys?"

"You shouldn't compare me to them."

"I'm a coach, Banks, it's what I do… C'mon, let's get some shots up," he says, jogging away.

I follow McCall as he crosses the blacktop. We pass the guy's court, and I stop, glaring, telling him, "I'd be careful how you assume that label of yourself."

"What's funny about that? …what are you staring at?"

"This here green grass, coach, between the courts, it's so beautiful, don't you agree?"

III.6

Mondays are when the school's front lawn reflects our brightest sunlight, but we can't touch it until after the last bell rings our freedom.

…we're jailed from journeying out there—kept inside to watch dust particles drift across empty space and between desks below the patterning punctured ceilings. I often switch over to the airplanes descending into P.A.X. above Uptown because I see them from the classroom window. They give dust particles the jet-engine thrusters needed to cross the classroom and land safely—somewhere—over there. Some are longer than others. Maybe they land on the extended runways.

But never where the leaves fall.

Neither where the rain drops.

And I'm never quite sure about the wind—

...ever so passing with my thoughts,

Often awaiting Thursday's trust.

But on a Friday, the last name, 'Banks,' somehow lands on the freshman roster. And by Saturday morning, I'm riding south beneath the Potomac for SouthStation. After three stops, I transfer at Jack London Square to ride southwest of the metropolitan and into Grossmont, where Lieberman High holds the annual kick-off jamboree. Joe' Prep saves on their transportation fund until the season starts. So, we get there when we get there...

I enter the east end of the carbon-domed gymnasium, where resting players and coaches stand between three side-by-side basketball courts. McCall and Maurice wave me to a corner where four other freshmen gather beside a wall bleacher at the west end of the gymnasium. McCall preaches as I approach, "When we step onto that court, I need all energy on me, your teammates, and more importantly, yourselves. I'll argue the whistles, so shut the entire fuck up— all game—okay? Banks, did you hear this? I'm fired up, boy; wow!"

Coach Maurice scratches his head and pulls out a fresh slice of gum. He chumps it like an over-seared tuna steak, bulging his temple veins and flexing his sharp, defined jawline muscles. "…keep your eyes on the wooden battlefield," he says. "We play to execute because winning ain't promised, but pain and hard work is. And remember what I say about selfishness; there's no *I* in 'team,' but there are two in 'winning' and 'quitting.' Put your teammates first; you put yourselves first."

McCall then asks, "Banks, can you do us a favor and tell each of your teammates walking in what we just said?"

"How?" I ask.

Coach Maurice snaps his fingers and pulls me aside, away from the other players. He spits his gum out and speaks sharply into my ear, "Do not question us after we ask you to do something."

"But I—"

"Because the next time you do, we will make an example out of you. Do we have this understanding?"

As four teammates approach our corner of the bleachers, I spray my first words, and it's Tokaiya, bending over to tighten his shoes. Yarnell scrolls through his L.D.S. before powering it off. Kenny rests his hands on his hips, watching the final minutes of the current game. Two other teammates, who I won't remember, go dead eyes on me and drool at the teeth.

Tokaiya walks over, asking, "So, bro, what are you talking

about?"

"I mean, it's what McCall says."

♦

♦

♦

Monday—McCall's text is an invite to his office for lunch—so I walk down at a quarter to noon.

"Sit. This won't be long," he says, clicking his pen. Twirling his pen. And tapping his pen against the desk. "Banks, I'm gonna need you to play clean ball this weekend. Exhibition time baby. They play fast, but you've got the vision. Did you speak to your father?"

"No. Not yet."

"And why not?"

"I don't know..."

"Let me ask," he says. "What battles back home were you personally facing?"

"Battles?"

"I know you don't pay attention in class, so think about the battles you'd be dealing with back home...instead of class."

"The people?"

"And who are they today?" he asks, nibbling his pen cap.

"They didn't come this way with us."

McCall drops his head, looking down past his beer-inflated belly. He scratches his goatee and powers on the monitor, asking, "Why do you think you're here?" He positions the screen to face me, and playing is the recording of Saturday's game-one tournament loss. He then places his ballpoint pen on the screen to where I'm dribbling the ball up court, circling the area of our offensive setup. "Take a mental snapshot of this," he says, ensuring I can see it. "And get used to this. But seriously, can you guess why you're here, in my office?"

"I'm expendable?"

"Did you just learn that word? Why'd you guess that?"

"Because I won't have parents in the stands who'll look at you funny after taking me out for turnovers?"

He laughs so hard that his pen drops, bouncing beneath his desk and landing beside my chair.

I don't dare look at it.

He can pick it up later.

Fuck that stupid pen.

"Care to guess again?" he asks.

"You said I'm fast, I have heart, and half the kids will either drop out or not have the grades to play?"

"If you execute as well as you're guessing and do exactly what I tell you... Focus your over-thinking brain in the right place, at the right time, and with good intentions, you'll get anywhere in this district."

"Alright."

"You and Tokaiya cool?"

"I think so. Why?"

McCall spins in his screeching chair and twirls another one of his stupid pens between his fingers. After four clicks off his tongue, he says, "You're playing with the varsity squad this Saturday."

"Okay. What about Tokaiya?"

"I'd be careful where you place your worries from now on," he winks. "You should be more concerned with what ol' man Gus says."

"You just said—."

"Never mind what people say. Your job is to trust yourself." McCall then examines the teeth marks he imprinted on a pen from this morning. "Wanna hear a joke?" he asks.

"Sure."

"Knock knock."

"Who's there?"

"Green."

"Green who?"

He smiles, grabs his rose water, and sprays the plants, responding, "Green grass, boy—."

JOURNAL IV

HIGH SCHOOL DAZE (CONT'D)

SUMMER... IT FEELS LONG AGO as the sky tumbles, making the last three years feel like right *now*. Colorful leaves make their way to the ground by the winds cutting through my jacket and raising the hairs along my arm. Crustation from my shins spread to my thighs, cracking across the pores of my belly and spreading like an infectious disease up my arms and hands. Dead skin shedding like the memories of *them* peels off my body and departs for a lone voyage through space— soon to find their way with the others beneath a couch or a bed.

Remember the monster's dustball?

It settles by gravity's fate. And if lucky, they'll see the fresh green grass again, or the stars above Laurent'co Circle twinkling the same green of a lawn I've yet to draw. But since the night skies of Port Avanti can only take me to the full Beaver MOON and back, stars don't dance across the dark canvasing sky—because people shine themselves—diluting GOD's nightly form of interstellar art.

·

·

I wonder what other kids do while I drown in my imaginary happy place all evening. Are they thinking about what pair of laced sneakers to buy?

I'm not.

They probably do homework.

I don't.

Maybe they help their parents with dinner?

I can't.

After the conversation with McCall, I arrive at our apartment, walking in as Gus awakens on the couch from a day of sleep. He lies on his back, untouchable, yet rubbing his unbearable eyes and grazing his rare grain of hair down to the scalp. Dandruff sheds across his pillow as he scratches his belly and rubs his crackling chest hairs that are thicker than the calluses on his feet. He moans. I kneel. We stare. So, I ask, "How do you grab it?"

"Grab it…" he says.

"A good feeling out there? You never seem down when it rains."

"When it rains, everyone gets wet," he says, rolling over to his side. His back faces me as he begins to hum… an unfamiliar rhythm. But maybe a melody I've slept through. Or a harmony we've lauded over the many Watchers of TheValleys. He then stops, coughs, and says, "When the SUN shines, some get burnt sooner than others."

"Who says that?" I ask. Gus turns back over, reaches for my ear, and rubs my right ear lobe. "What's that for?"

"They've been painting ears on you kids. And I hate wasting my breath."

"But I can hear you."

He tries poking at my eyeball with his middle finger, but I flinch. "Good," he says. "Do you do that with the SUN?"

"What, look at it?"

"Do you question what's shining?"

"No."

"Then you should know what to watch for."

"But in basketball—"

"Your muse," he interrupts, giggling around his patronizing tongue. There's a hole in the side of the couch where I poke my finger through, anticipating he'll further explain himself. But he slaps my hand away from the hole, blowing childish air bubbles from his lips. "Remember the aromas from the gardens our Watchers were healed? So strong and…man, even our crofters felt the *business*. But it's you and I, moving up, as ourselves. Did you hear?"

"I can hear you."

"Remember at night when we lit up the flares and blinded everyone? We blocked moonlight for a reason. Like in Tola and Vizala?"

"Okay?"

"You listen to react?"

"But I can hear you."

"You're hearing the *light of our last*," he praises.

It's moments like this where Gus speaks from his majestic tongue, confusing me at a time when I turn to the most amusing thing in sight. It's moments like this where our ceiling opens up, the television brightens, and his incense lights itself—burning aromas that'll forever penetrate our brown living-room carpet. "What's your need?" he asks. "My alarm hasn't even gone off."

"Well, what did you tell my basketball coach?"

"Oh my... That guy?" Gus laughs. And finally, he sits up. "You know, he reminds me of Nwaka. But with a better upbringing."

"He reminded me to talk to you."

"...because some of us would rather lead in hell than serve in heaven."

"I don't know what that means."

"It means people have choices."

"What choices?" I ask.

"How they lead. You're choosing to lead, but only if you feel good?"

"Yeah, so, how do you grab it? I'm starting in Saturday's varsity exhibition game."

"Sorry, I must miss it."

"But there'll be at least two thousand Avantian kids watching."

"At an exhibition?"

"And coaches will put me back on the freshmen team with Tokaiya if I don't play well. So, how'd you do it?"

"I was never competing," he says. "You would never understand how I find a 'good' feeling."

"But you led the people."

"Yes. Until I understood how to be quiet and listen for it."

"Listen for what?"

"You're a humming being. Shut up for long enough, and you'll hear it."

"But what about the pictures in my head?"

Gus laughs so hard that he slaps the couch, shouting, "SMACK!" and throws his blanket onto the floor. He gets up from the sofa and heads for the kitchen but somehow leaves his legs across the sofa's armrest. He shouts from the hallway, "You a...*muse* me by what you want to hear."

I lie in bed while Gus chants over the running waters of his shower, reminiscing about the Spring tides over our communal fires and flares launching at every full MOON up high. I ponder what his dreams entail. I wonder if his mind speaks in ways of divine direction. And if so, what were his illusions of choice—because he could've told me to fuck off.

The shower cuts off, and his singing continues. Gus leaves the bathroom and pokes his head through my doorway. "And just remember," he says. "Your muse…it competes with no one."

"But this is basketball."

"It's with ten people, right?"

"Yes. Five on five."

"Then bringing your *best* game won't be good enough," he says. "You gotta muse into your *beast*. That's where your 'A' game is played. Can you picture that?"

♦

When falling asleep, images in my head appear individually, each emerging like a slideshow or roll of film. Sometimes, the images play out like a movie, whether I want them to or not. Long ago, I pictured Port Avanti, an ambiance built on the Atlantic Coast shorelines capped by rows of clustering skyscrapers. I pictured each skyscraper tickling the above gaping skies so our modern-day architects' creations poke through the fog come autumn. I pictured his glowing sources of light probing further above our biosphere as each is set within Earth's low orbit to radiate year-round. And by confusing future generations about what a real star is up there, beneath those lights and atop each building, I pictured colorful illuminations, strobing to attract TheDistrict's advancement in technology.

But I couldn't picture the people who'd come here for freedom after arriving upon the shores of contentment—the land of the future—through the airways of solvency—soon to understand that an elephant will actually eat the brown grass of sorrow. And I couldn't have pictured the role I'd be playing in TheDistrict's curriculum, where on my most critical days of learning, I'd pay just as much attention to the buttons missing on my teammate's shirt.

IV.2

"Rigil. You must stay awake in my class," says Ms. Bradshaw's face. And she's irked, kneeling at desk level with my resting head. She leans into my face as she wipes her lenses, whispering, "Can you sit up? Or do you need to stand?"

"No, I can listen."

"How am I supposed to know that if you're sleeping?"

"Won't we have a test on it?"

"Yes, but that doesn't mean you can sleep on my lecture.

Can you repeat what I just spoke about?"

I sit up from my desk and scan the classroom. The carbon ViDi screen board up front is blurry, so I squint to make out her drawings and diagrams. "No, that's okay."

Ms. Bradshaw catches her jaw before it hits the top of my desk. "You don't decide that," she says. "Let's get up. You know my rule; if you sleep, you speak."

"*You just made that shit up.*"

"It's all on the board," she insists. "I'll give you three minutes to paraphrase."

"Para' of what?"

"Tell me what you learned from my lesson. And take your time."

And so, I stand. I exhale. I take each step down to the front of the class with care and caution because it must be *me* who presents to these students. However, while my back is turned to everyone, I face the screen board and, "*Interesting…*"

So, I ask Ms. Bradshaw, "Egypt?"

"That is correct," she says, crossing her legs across the aisle from my desk.

I continue standing, dumbfounded and barefaced-stoned in front of a class, all at full attention. I count four breaths until I notice one kid in the third row, who also draws—isn't paying attention. The girl one seat over is so eager to hear the words off my tongue, that she drools over her SpacePad, not noticing the boy behind her playing footsy wars with the straps of her purse beneath her desk. "Can you see the board okay?" Ms. Bradshaw asks. "Do you need glasses?"

"No. But I'm about to speak."

"Great. The floor is yours."

"Okay, so, are these pyramids?" I ask, pointing to the triangles on the corner of the screen board.

"Yes," Ms. Bradshaw responds.

"Where are the ones with steps?"

"What's that got to do with my lesson?"

"That wasn't in your lesson?" I ask.

Ms. Bradshaw turns to the class. "Now, do you see what happens when you don't pay attention? Anyone who sleeps on my lesson will be exactly where you stand."

"Okay. Am I done? Am I done being your example?"

She places her hand on her chin, uncrosses her legs, and walks to the board. "Does this period of time look familiar?" she asks, pointing toward the end of the board where she wrote out date ranges and a lineage of names.

"That's when they messed up. Doj—" But I stop…curious of everyone watching Ms. Bradshaw.

The classroom suddenly opens up in laughter, projecting their vocals off the windows in unison with the others who're throwing their humor bones against the walls. Each of their voices… penetrating my eardrums and pounding my canal walls until swelling the right side of my brain. The burning up my throat pokes at the bottom of my tongue—moving with the giggling gestures of these bastard-looking students. Whatever's in my throat moves back down and boils the lining of my stomach. Ms. Bradshaw puts her hand up at the class, begging them to quiet down. "At least I know most of you have been listening," she says. She then approaches my side, whispering, "Djoser and the ones near it will be a big part of tomorrow's lesson, okay?"

I take my seat, and the vigorous boil in my stomach moves decisively back up my esophagus. Some call it heartburn, indigestion, or acid reflux—but for me, it's the monster—disturbed by a tyrant's tongues. So, I stand, covering my mouth as the first dry heave pulsates my chest. I rush to the front of the class as the second dry heave jerks my neck. "Rigil, are you okay?" Ms. Bradshaw asks. I get seven feet from the trash and stumble, falling stomach first to the floor. About an ounce makes it up my throat and reaches my uvula—enough to swallow back down as I crawl the last few inches, reaching for the trash can and…SPLAT.

I pour the first colorful bile of avocado bean burgers, tater tots, and oatmeal muffins into the trash. The second spout of bile rushes past the back of my tongue like an unhinged water hose, filling the bottom lining of the garbage.

Several kids in the front row grab their backpacks and rush toward the back of the class as I inhale, heave, inhale, and then launch the big one. Ms. Bradshaw crouches to my side, rubbing my back as the last bit is jerked from the back of my throat. She hands me a wet washcloth from a student who rinsed it in the sink.

I grab it. I wipe my hands. I wipe my mouth. I then hold both ends of the trash bag open to take a final look at the colorful array of regurgitated stars—the light of my lids— sitting chunky and lumpy as it radiates fumes of a yuck mouth across a repulsed room full of kids.

It's warm.

It's heavy.

Some parts are green.

Other parts are purple.

Most of it's brownish.

...looking as though someone artistically spilled a mixture of luminous finger paint into the trash. I stare long enough for half the kids to watch me in awe, shocked—yet amused as no one's begun recording this moment where me and my inner sourced phosphenes have a moment of...

Ms. Bradshaw pulls on a pair of sanitary gloves, walks over, and reaches for the bag, but I slap her hand away. I snatch the bag out of the trash bin and place my hand beneath the plastic liner and walk it to the back of the class, watching everyone cover their nose, except a kid who says, "Take that shit out back." It's Tokaiya, who I didn't see when I first stood up front. His head turns in disgust as I exit the door. But honestly, I hadn't noticed him until he said that.

I reenter the school through the brown-walled halls and take a right at the green hall, but not the flagged walls because then I'd be lost en route to help. Tokaiya walks aggressively toward me—faster and faster—and suddenly rushes against my left shoulder to shout in my ear, "You think you the shit now, bruh?" I peek down and take a liking to his laced sneakers. They're nice. But my eyes make their way back up to his hat. "You can see me now, huh, boy?"

He steps closer, sneering beneath my nose and flaring his nostrils. "What's this got to do with?" I ask.

"Don't play me. Stupid."

I leap back. He steps closer. And the mist from his breath turns my face as I head the other direction, counting three breaths while saying, "I'm going to my locker. I'm not sure what you want."

Kids begin pulling out their L.D.S., recording as he rushes to impede my steps. "What did you say?" he shouts. "No one can ever hear you."

I exhale. I turn around. And he brushes against my

backpack, yelling nonsense at the side of my cheek. "Walk the other way, Tokaiya..."

"You scared?"

"You're not the bigger man."

He shoves me with his chest, pinning me against the beige lockers so I can't move. I shove him off, and he loses his balance, falling into three students. He attempts to catch himself, but his right arm whips through one recording student's arm, smacking their phone to the floor, and it shatters.

"Yo, yo, cut the shit," shouts our junior D1 prospect, Howard Conlin. He towers through a crowd of students with his notebook held up high in one hand, raising the split at the bottom of his shirt where he visibly missed a button.

Tokaiya pants, walking away and screaming, "Fuck this kiss ass no-name."

Howard stands. His eyes wide shut. Confused and startled—surrounded by students recording the aftermath. "What was that about?" Howard asks.

"I don't know."

"At least one of you was the bigger man and walked away."

"I, actually said that."

◆

◆

◆

I get home, and Remi's in the room reading. I toss my backpack across the bed and continue through the hall. Her book drops to the floor just as I enter the kitchen for almonds. While reaching for the top shelf, she coughs through the hallway. "I heard Dad on the phone with McCall earlier," she says. The container tips over from the top shelf, spilling dozens of almonds that fall to the floor and scatter beneath the table. "Why don't you slow down?" she says.

"Where's the broom?"

Remi takes a seat at the table and helps with a couple of almonds off the floor. "You can still eat these. Just don't eat too much. Dad left you soup and salad in the refrigerator."

"Because of my stomach?"

"What? No. Your Freshman woes."

"What's that?"

"My friends were talking about your fight in the halls. Did you get my message?"

"Yes."

"Why didn't you respond?"

"Because my stomach didn't feel well."

"So, he did hit you?"

"No. That's not what he did."

"So how come you didn't respond?" she asks.

"Wow, Remi, look at all these almonds, okay?"

"You're being an asshole. You better have it together

before the game on Saturday."

"The game's canceled."

"Whatever," she says. "Don't let everyone get to you; they'll talk about it at school tomorrow."

"School's also canceled."

"'Wait. You're suspended?"

IV.3

FIVE YEARS AGO—BHAVANA

This is Summer's Mission: a missionary movement out of the Americas established to protect VILLAGEROCK'S Valleys—implementing the mark of global technologies, improving third-world literacy, and a general sense of social awareness.

On an afternoon when our SUN hangs hot, leaving the grounds to be a stove, Vinetra, the tech guru, gathers her eleven kids, including myself, and instructs us to sit in a circle. While some of us are on our knees, me, I'm flexible, sitting cris cross applesauce at the opening of the circle. Vinetra ensures we're spread far enough apart and tells each of us there's no talking, just whispering to the next kid when spoken to. I'm selected as her first point of contact, so she shows me a phrase she wrote on a piece of paper—and once I understand it, I whisper it to Gavin. And so, that's what I do, and Gavin tells it to the next kid. The written message I first whispered transfers from mouth to ear, one soul at a time.

While some kids need to hear it twice, others take it and tell. I see kids confused, questioning their ability to comprehend the English *they've* drilled into our heads under the pearly white tints beneath Pavilion Three. Eventually, the message circulates back around and whispered into the ear of the girl on my left. Vinetra tells her to keep the message to herself so she can tell the group what she heard from the boy on her left. As the girl stands, she looks at me and says, "Milky sweat for the elephants?".

The circle of kids begins chuckling in unifying laughter, even Vinetra. But it's me who she watches—closely by her fading laughter as she squints, studying my dry face. She kneels, asking, "What's wrong, Ahliko?"

"That's not what I said to him."

♦

This is Summer's Mission, where the Big Men of VillageRock send their kids to work on the lands of Nigeria's TrenchPort Valleys through June and July. In August, the privileged teenagers pack up to return to their homelands of lavender and oak, milk and honey, and wheats with apples.

One Friday night, beneath tint number one, a green tint, we watch the roaring lion at the beginning of a movie. From across the main pavilion in tint number eight, a black tint, the helix-shaped logo for Yanaka-Beta 3.2 lights up the monitor of workstation three. The laptop's standby mode must've been triggered off, emitting light across pavilions two and three as bright as a 4X4's headlight. However, the light is distorted by the Acacias we planted at the center of the campsite, giving a long protrusion of shadows over our dead Daphnes and Tulips that'll rebloom with the Acacia come spring.

I walk the clay-paved path bordered by the browning grass around the campsite, stepping through the gardens and beneath a pavilion where snacks are served with the flies.

No one sees me.

No one hears me—

...dreaming of arriving at a new star over yonder, past our yellowish Pink Supermoon, and beyond a lighthouse where citizens would await my arrival.

...thinking

building...

I also play with the images in my head, soon to be configured, projected, and then manifested on a screen.

I feel the goodness of this vision—like a fresh bite into a mango—soothing airwaves soaking up my ear canals—as though the drummers and vocalists would celebrate our Watcher's return from a victorious war for space.

I sit at workstation three, pulled by the revelations of comfort where the kids can eat without TheDistrict's PhatCats being incentivized to write it off. The women can clean without wiping slowly through overtime pay hours. The feeling of abundance, prosperity, and service is contagious with only a smile. Fumes from the searing fields are instead, our noble scribes burning the midnight oil—because our people have a story worth sharing for generations.

.

.

"Ahliko, are you sleeping? Can you hear me?" Suntanned arms, freckled hands, and crusted fingers shake my shoulders. "Someone, I need help." It's Vinetra, shouting out the entryway of the black tech tint. Her right hand is planted against her forehead, panting and holding up my head.

A shadowy figure scurries to the opening outside the tint and fingers through his hair. He's confused. They both are. But the camp director rushes to my side, pressing his hand against my chest, "Lie back down," he says. "You're safe here."

I remain on the bean bag mat, listening to Vinetra stutter, "I thought we lost you."

"Did he pass out?" the director asks.

"I... came in, and he was just lying here," she responds.

"Ahliko, who let you in the tint?"

Tongue-tied whatsoever, Vinetra's flailing eyes plead, "Are you just now waking up?"

I look to my left. And glance to my right. "He's not

responding," says the director. "I'll get a medic."

I reach for Vinetra's laptop, and she brushes my hand away. "What are you doing? Can you talk? Have you eaten?"

"Yeah, before the movie."

"What movie?" she asks.

"In the green tint."

"Yes, film night was Friday with the kids. Did you eat this morning before sneaking in here?"

"This morning?" I ask.

The director and a medic return, injecting me with an IV full of droplets falling through a tube. Each drop is shot into my left arm's vein, bringing a vile secretion of saliva coating the walls of my mouth.

After five minutes, Vinetra and I are left alone with a lukewarm breeze through the tint's opening. The local clan of singing cicadas orchestrate the distorted frequencies between us, harmonizing with the whistling brown feather grass across the campsite. "So, what's up?" Vinetra asks. "You're not going to tell us what's been going on in that brain of yours?"

"Your voice."

"My what?"

"You," I respond. "White noise." Vinetra opens her jaw, palming her ears all the way down to her mouth with both hands. "You always tell me what your people say while we're doing Yanaka on the workstations."

"You actually listen to my stories?" she asks. "What do you remember?"

"Everything."

"You haven't told anyone, have you?"

The director returns and immediately examines workstation three—sensing the monitor fan blowing hot air against the back of his hand. "Why is this on?" he asks.

"He must've been here for a while," Vinetra responds.

"Ahliko," says the director, "This is Summer's Mission, where kids cannot be alone in a tint at any time, for any reason. Okay? Does your father know you left this morning?"

"This morning?" I ask.

"Yes," he responds. "Today is Sunday, and our tech tint is closed on the weekends. Did you sneak out last night?"

"We should wait for the medic to come back," Vinetra suggests. "He doesn't even know what day it is."

The director exits, leaving Vinetra and me alone. So, I ask, "Why are you ashamed of your skin?"

She looks me in my eye, fluttering her eyelashes but with an off-guarded laugh, "I am not," she says. "You couldn't be any more random in the mornings."

"But I thought about it—"

"And it's not that I'm ashamed. It's complicated. You kids are lucky to have that SUN shining all year."

"It didn't shine yesterday."

"Did you bother to look up?" she asks. "For someone who needs it, like me, these Valleys are just what a girl needs."

"Why is that?"

"For my skin. TheDistrict doesn't get much sunshine all year."

"Port Avanti?" I ask. Instead of responding, Vinetra pulls out her phone and drops her head. She scrolls through a phenomenon of cityscape photos, skylines above a fresh green lawn on an oceanfront shore, and views of sidewalks with shops on the first levels of buildings spawning from the concrete. I feel her drift further from our moment—further than the strip of blue skylight splitting the towers at the top of her photos. So, I ask again, "Port Avanti? Is that Port Avanti?"

"Yeah, but this part is hell."

"Because it's hot? Is that why you're sweating?"

"No. But it's like how you felt after the game of telephone."

"So, you're mad now? Are you mad at Port Avanti?" I ask.

"Why do you ask so many questions?"

"I hear life is meaningless."

"…you heard?"

"Yeah. And we have to ask questions to get meaningful answers."

"That's interesting. But you can't always believe

everything you hear."

"But Gus said it out loud."

"And are you repeating what I say out loud?" she asks.

The director returns with the medic to have the IV needle removed from my arm. They help me off the bean bag mat and onto my feet, ensuring I stand well and balanced. The medic instructs me to walk to the tint's entryway and back—and then out toward the pavilions. Vinetra remains inside the tint while the director, medic, and I stand outside the black tech tint beneath our blistering SUN. I shade my eyes with my hand as the SUN burns directly across the surface of my sclera whites and through the protruding sockets of my corneas. "Must've been good sleep," says the director. "And was your father watching you when you left this morning?" he asks.

"This morning?"

"Did you come from your home?" the director asks.

"He mentioned something about a movie around here," says the medic.

The director responds, "Yeah, that's where the Gavin kid last saw him. But there's no way. We had three supervisors that night."

"Are they around?" the medic asks.

With every flourishing ego Vinetra lures into from her divisive virtual village, time passes at the edges of her fingers as she peruses her phone with mad thumbs.

…her moment delusional,

and reality deceptive.

"Was she one of your supervisors Friday night?" the director asks.

"Shrugs"

And he repeats, "Did she say any of you could be in that tint at any point Friday evening?"

I respond, "No, not anyone."

"Then who?"

"Only special kids—like me."

IV.4

HIGH SCHOOL DAZE (CONT'D)

Lying in bed and home for the day suspended, my first thought of the morning is the guilt of sleep. Well past my alarm clock and into the dawn of daylight, the green grass of Harmon's Terrace turns. I know the SUN will inevitably shine, but only above the nimbostratus haze of a sky so dull—so shy. Ashes of memories could ascend through those smokey grey clouds as they drift, float, and cover the city as though they, too, fear the drop of a tear.

In anticipation of Gus returning from his night shift in Uptown, the monster thumps against my sternum, fueling the inevitable conversations taking space in my head.

Our front door sounds off, and Gus enters through the living room walkway. His footsteps crackle both sides of our

baseboards down the hallway as he passes my room—which calms my heart rate as the crackling trickles into the kitchen.

It's quiet.

It's calm.

It's serene,

As though a storm brews,

And then it's Gus, entering my room. "You and your teammate doing alright?" he asks. "What's going on?" He stares. He putters. And ponders at the floor. "Anything you want to share with me about yesterday?"

"My stomach was hurting."

"What does that have to do with you and that Japanese-black kid? Isn't he a teammate?"

"No, hallmate. Tokaiya hasn't liked me since seventh grade."

"But there's video of you pushing him into another child."

"That was my reaction."

"So he did hit you?"

"No. He shoved me into the wall, and my stomach wasn't feeling good."

"So, why not go to the nurse's office?"

"Because he pushed me into the lockers on the way."

"Ahli, control your tone. This isn't what they showed me."

"I'm telling you now, out loud."

"Again, your tone," Gus warns. "Why not tell someone at school?"

"Because they all watched me."

"Watched you?"

"Yes, when I threw up."

"You threw up?"

"I just said that. Out loud."

"And where was your teacher?" he asks.

"Being a bitch."

Gus storms into the kitchen and returns, holding up a steak knife. "Open up and say ah," he says.

"What's that for?"

"Our mother tongue doesn't speak of souls as such."

"What?"

Gus reaches for my jaw, "Did they grow you a new tongue? Open up," he says.

"Who?" I holler, running toward my room. He follows me halfway through the hall, and fortunately, I hear him place the knife back into the holder.

"Either you or that tongue of yours needs to go," he shouts from the kitchen.

"Where?"

"Outside. Go."

"But where?" I ask. "And why?"

"Just leave."

"But where should I go?"

"You'll see. Just go…pass the boys high off boogers and sucking up dead hey."

"What's that?"

"Introduce yourself, and they'll tell you."

Tension between us looms to the front door, where he slams it on the heels of my feet, rushing me further down the steps.

"Hey, hold on," Gus shouts from the doorway. He marches down the steps, holding out a brown bag.

"What's that?" I ask.

"Almonds, oats, and granola," he says, placing the bag against my chest. "The grapes are for your stomach."

"How long am I supposed to be gone for?"

"Just be quiet," he winks. "If you can't do that? Close your eyes and watch," then he rushes back into the apartment. He leaves me alone with a brown bag of aged organics and room-temperature fruit weighing heavy at the bottom.

I walk the Harmon's Terrace parking lot until grazing a row of solar panels at the complex entrance. Dreary rainfall continues to soak the straps of my sneakers while glistening the palettes of dusky lawn fronts. From this block on, grey clouds smother the hidden blue above, surrounding our neighboring blocks like a mural of depression. As I approach the second block, there stands no one to meet, no one to see.

> But I stop,
> I stare,
> And breathe,
> …as Lone Avenue awaits.

JOURNAL V

SATURDAY—DAY THREE

FRIDAY NIGHT AROUND 2:30AM, a car horn squeals throughout the neighborhood from a street below. The echoes bounce off the concrete walls of the three-story coffee shop on Grant Street and pulsate up the metal side panels of our building. I jump out of bed and look down from my writing nook, and at the three-way intersection of 66th and Knolls, two cars are stopped in the middle of the street. One lady is letting it fly, flipping her wig, furious at the other driver who remains in his car. "You weren't even paying attention," she shouts. Her voice projects over the two-story apartment complex and ascends above rooftops like steam rising out of sewers. "Are you stupid?" she screams as the man sits protected behind the window of his car. He shrugs, seemingly in fear of the enraged lady whose palms pound against his door handle—so loud that her thumping crawls up the vertical windowpanes of the tower and vibrates into my apartment. The rainfall creates a spare of white noise that blankets the ruckus, causing havoc through my ears drums.

If I walk away from the window, I can count the raindrops tapping against my window until falling asleep. If I stay watching, I can witness the man finally stepping out of his car and being attacked by the enraged woman shouting in his ear as he calmly opens his umbrella.

And so I sip my water and stir in a freshly squeezed lemon as the guy hands the woman his umbrella. He crawls into the mad woman's car and reaches beneath the steering wheel as she waits beside the door. After 20 seconds of oncoming traffic detouring around them through the intersection, the car horn is disarmed. The guy gets out, grabs his umbrella from the woman, walks back to his car, and drives off. He leaves the woman stranded, standing soaked as she shouts every curse word from the Avantian vocabulary— yelling things no one should say aloud, especially to adults.

Eventually, it's Saturday morning—day three—another spring morning where I just don't care. I just don't know. Why am I here? And feeling so empty—fading unalive. The meaningless art on my walls makes my apartment look like a vacation condo. I could get a cat. But I like my leather sofa. And I love my pool tables. It's the one piece of furniture that rarely collects dust. I play... sometimes. But only when the monster challenges me to a game of dust-ball.

I make it down to our courtyard just as Deliah's crew gets set up near the concierge desk. Perkins shuffles a stack of papers, wearing a silk buttoned crew neck with his pants legs rolled up—showing off his mid-top Oxfords and baby-oiled ankles. He's throttled the smell goods around his neck, but now it's the lotion glistening his thick forearm hairs surrounding the gold links on his watch. "What's all this?" I ask.

Perkins continues to shuffle the forms like a deck of cards. He eyes Deliah as she approaches, straightening her fitted top and Capri bottoms. "Sheesh," he says, catching my glare. "Save it for the dirty shirt." He rolls his eyes, stiffens his back, and turns away from Deliah—but leaves the forms on the corner of his desk.

"Those are the four slips I'll need you to sign," Deliah points.

"Why four?" I ask.

"You didn't sign them yesterday," she smiles.

"Okay. What about the completion request? And what's he doing?" I point toward Guala, who's slumped on our lobby bench with his head drooping up and down over his lap.

"I'll bring the updated completion request on Monday."

"Monday?" I ask. Deliah nudges Guala's shoulder so hard that he has to catch himself from falling on the plastic covering of the carpet. He speaks up, but I can't understand his response as he points toward the storage shed latch.

"He's just apologizing and doing the best he can."

"Okay, but that 'day of completion' form, can you bring it tomorrow?"

"We don't work Sundays."

"Perk'," I shout. "Did you call to reschedule the appraisers?"

"And I'm curious," Deliah ponders. "Does the appraiser need that form?"

"It's a good business gesture, especially when everything's on sale. But is Guala gonna be alright? It's not even nine o'clock."

"He's doing his best. We're working doubles after picking up another project in Grossmont."

"Grossmont?" I respond. "Yuck…doesn't our contract have a loyalty clause?"

Deliah steps back, resting against the corner of our concierge desk, but carelessly swipes her work order forms onto the floor. "If you're concerned that'll interfere with this, believe me, I've managed four moving projects at once with these guys."

"And with delays?"

"Delays are part of the business," she claims. "And considering it rained last night…"

"But what about our agreement? I didn't know you wouldn't be working on Sunday."

"It's in our work orders. Did you read them?"

"The ones on the floor?"

"Did I just do that," she says, gathering the forms off the carpet as though she's lost her marbles.

"I'd like to not worry about anyone sleeping on site. So, can I trust you all to do your part? Just like I trust Perkins to tell me everything that's going on when I'm not around the courtyard?"

Perkins pulls the phone away from his ear, visibly irked. "Why would you bring me into this?" he asks.

"Because we always double-check the storage's lock latch, right?"

"This tension," says Deliah. "Only puts us further behind."

"Tension?" I ask.

"Yes, tension."

"Tension, like—"

"Have you lost your tusks or something?" she asks. "We need you to be serious."

Perkins has his eyebrows raised higher than the pitch of his silent mouthing, saying, "Wow…"

"What's with the look?" I ask, pointing directly at his dramatic fucking face.

"Young man," says Perkins. "Do not point that finger at my face like that. And the appraiser will get back to us on a new date."

"Okay, but please," Deliah begs. "Can you do your part by reading and signing these work orders as soon as you get a hold of a pen? We do business old school; technology can be iffy, ya' know?"

My favorite pen sits beside a spray can of Oxford shoe polishing oil in the concierge desk drawer. I grab the pen, sign Deliah's stupid forms, place the pen on Perkins' countertop, and walk away. "Can't you put it back yourself?" Perkins asks.

But I leave it.

As I turn the corner to our elevator bank walkway, I look back, and the pen, it's still next to Perkins, who's sharing the wrinkles on the back of his hairy middle finger.

V.2

HIGH SCHOOL DAZE (CONT'D)

I venture up Lone Avenue next to its glistening decommissioned street rail as raindrops follow my every step to the city's echoing sirens, whistling hydro-rails, and thudding dew drops across the SuperChannel's pavement. I gaze through the fog as a rustic neon-edged coffee shop flickers an *'Open 24/7'* sign once, twice, and then once again but thrice more. It flashes so welcoming, with a retrograde palm tree that I brush against through the entrance. There's a gift shop to the right of their squeaking floorboard just before entering the dining area. Inundated train models dangle from the ceiling by thin threads next to polished train tracks and cut-out shapes of glass mirrors reflecting my open-mouth fisheye. "Yo', I can take your order when you're ready," says the baristo from the back room.

"What do you have?"

"We have a menu," he says. "Where are you coming from?"

"Harmon's Terrace."

"So, you live around here?"

"Yeah. What are the mirrors?" I ask.

"Those are the nine states, bro. They're cut into the Avantian states. Found them in rubbish after *them* people went crazy all over the Parish."

"They went crazy?"

"Yes... Where are you from?"

"Do you know TrenchPort Valleys?"

"That's—."

"It's over there."

"I know where it's at," he says, laughing between the

ether of us. But his humor dies. His eyes fade. And he repositions his hat, stuffing his wool head of hair beneath it. "I guess whatever you want, it's all on the house," he says.

"How much is that?"

"As you be, free."

"I don't see your water."

"It's on our SolarShelf."

"Do you have lemons?" I ask.

Their coin tray opens as he fingers my order into their digital till. He then shoves it closed with his hip. "Man, I've always wanted to travel over there. My LEIP will increase soon, so I can plan my next five years, at least. That's if I don't end up reenlisting."

"My dad's getting his soon."

"So, ya'll ain't been here long?"

"Just a couple of years."

"Do you like it over here better?"

"Well, we moved a lot. It was part of my dad's work."

"Was he military?"

"No. He built communities."

"Word? I don't know anything about real estate."

"Neither did he."

"But to build over there is what? I hear it's cheap."

"It wasn't the suburbs."

"Oh, of course," he says. "Africa is huge."

"Africa?"

"Yes, you're from Africa?"

"TrenchPort."

"Africa?" he repeats.

"Ummm."

"Bro, what?"

"But where are you from?"

"Nahant Beach," he says. "TheDistrict's northern border. But I grew up in Blotsburg."

"Why did you come here?"

"My mom got assigned to program the machines that built the GTube brake systems."

"Did your dad come with you?"

"Not necessarily. He plays the sax, and that's what he chose."

A couple enters, a man and a woman, and the baristo waves me to step aside. I grab a water bottle from their SolarShelf and head to a single bar stool table facing the window. I pull off my backpack and immediately stuff my mouth with a handful of mixed organics from the bag. The grains dry my salivating mouth. But the grapes make it easy to chew. And the water is like a perfect fountain of trust washing it all down…

But then…spillage,

It drips onto my shirt.

And that guy, he coughs.

The gloom from outside helps reflect the couple's curiosity from behind as he coughs twice more. But I mind my own, squeezing a lemon into my water.

Basking in this passé coffee shop, I rest my chin on the tabletop, watching clouds aggressively conceal the skyline of Uptown. But somewhere within, seeing where I'd belong, this city couldn't be hell unless it's me musing beyond the edges of conditional thinking spaces—where dust floats—or me, breathing above the norms of a city well designed.

Although I can't see how, I feel—so...

From here, shall my journey of thoughts come into reality as they've grown from cruelty to ask: who am I off the trenches where birth was shammed? And to answer: I'll be down there one day, cashing more than just a check.

"You good, bro?" the baristo asks. "We're short-staffed. I gotta close for my lunch. If you don't have anywhere to go, come back in an hour."

As I'm strapping on my backpack, the couple exits into the gift shop. *"...the fuck y'all lookin' at?"*

The woman trips while facing to turn the corner—but she's caught by the man before stumbling into the store rack.

"White women," the baristo laughs. "Always nosey..."

But it takes three trains, two transfers, and one fool to meet the most intrusive.

♦

♦

♦

…at Jamla's Bar and Grill—she sits, waiting at a booth table for four between two imported palm trees wrapped in slow flashing lights. The surrounding carpet is orange, and the ceiling is a contrasting blue. Not sky blue, but a dirty textured river blue. The type of blue you see if all the restaurant's food waste was dumped into an island's cove somewhere in the Caribbean and mixed with the conspicuous tourist trash. Remi enters the booth first, sliding her bottom across the seat and stopping to sit beside the lady. I slide in after Remi as Gus takes the end seat of the booth. And then Remi… she turns, taps my shoulder, and gently points for Gus and me to slide back out. So we crawl out of the booth, gather ourselves, and it's me—sliding in first to be next to this lady, who sits across from Gus as they occupy the ends of the booth table. "What do we eat here," Gus asks, exhaling his exhaustion. "And what are they doing with this silverware? Freeze drying? For why?"

"I take it you don't eat salads," says Shauren. Her name is Shauren. "It's not as 'urban' as some of the places near you guys, but I bet you two will love the food," she assumes.

Remi fingers the bread, spreading oil and softened butter on each side of her slice. Gus stares, asking, "What is this? You've had this before?"

"Yeah," Remi responds. "It's pumpernickel."

"But that's black."

"Gus, you should try it," Shauren suggests. "I told you I wanted to show you something new."

"I don't know," says Gus. "Not sure I like my bread darker than me."

Gus grabs his wine glass and makes a silent toast with Shauren as she sniffs around the rim. She rests the glass below her nose and raises it to her eyes for another sniff. And there… I watch a delegator of others who teach tools to fools—like me. She's a bit perky, upbeat, and quick to respond. I don't know what Gus sees in this lady besides her dark gray jumpsuit, gold gauntlet, and warm autumn boots. But maybe it's the blackened bread of sorrow she's led him to.

"Rigil, are you ready to order?" Shauren asks.

"The salad and clam chowder, please."

"That's all?" she says. "Do you see their pan pizza, sautéed shrimp, and I bet you love steak?"

"Just keep the tab open for him," says Gus. "He'll be eating like an elephant in no time."

Shauren downs her wine and sets the half-drank glass beside our bread, asking Remi, "You're going to be a senior next year?"

"Yep. Then I'm thinking about enlisting."

"In the Military?" Shauren asks, skewing her head.

"Yeah."

"My brother joined. And it tore our family apart after the...you know?"

"Why?" Remi asks.

"We knew he was doing it for the money. Then had to take sides after the acquittals."

"Ha," Gus chuckles.

"...as long as you know what you want," Shauren responds.

"Why say it like that?" Remi asks.

"Well, with my brother, he finished boot camp and got stationed overseas."

"That's what I want," Remi says, gazing at the trees. "I want to travel more. Where'd your brother go?"

"He can never tell us. But hey, sky's the limit if you know how to take advantage of the opportunities."

"Sounds like a normal job to me," Gus mumbles.

"It's like college, but 2.0," says Remi.

"But what about the military attracts you?" Shauren asks.

Remi's eyes veer up. And mine do the same. But me, I finally notice the seaweed wrapping around the hanging recessed lights. Some of the seaweed looks dry. Others have enough lighting angled on them to reflect a gloss against the discoloration. "I have a friend who almost joined," says Remi. "They went through the recruiting process but got scared at the last minute."

Gus sets his wine glass down. "Who's this friend?" he asks.

"And be careful around others who are trigger-shy," Shauren winks.

"Remilee, who is your friend?" Gus repeats. "Who's already been through recruitment?"

"We're young," she says. "We can make mistakes. Better now than later, right?"

Gus responds, "But who are you following? Are they your age?"

"No one. And I have plenty of time to think about it."

"They're growing up," says Shauren. "Get used to it." She then sips her wine and plants both hands on the table, mumbling, "He just better be cute."

Gus lifts his lap napkin, throws it onto the table, grabs a piece of bread, and storms toward the bathroom.

"But he's just a friend," Remi exhales.

"Don't mind him," says Shauren. "When I was your age, my father reacted exactly like him. Most men can't handle the thought of their princess being taken from them by some random guy. At least until they meet. And what about you, Rigil? I know girls have their eyes on you playing ball."

"Ha," Remi laughs, covering her mouth.

"Nothing was funny, was it?" I ask.

"Not at all," Remi responds.

"Maybe he's not interested in girls," says Shauren.

Remi drops her jaw to the gradient borders of the orange and blue carpet beneath the table, daring me... "Wow," she says, punching my knee. "Why don't you say anything? Speak up."

"I get it," says Shauren, finishing her wine. "I have a cousin just like you. Soo mysterious..."

I place my lap napkin across the table, face Remi, and point gently away from Shauren. Remi rolls her eyes, but still, she slides out of the booth table to let me out. I walk to the entrance and wait at the hand-carved log bench for the time it takes me to become the person who knows not to say the things a boy should not say aloud to adults.

.
.

After three train rides and two transfers of silence, we're off a late evening GTube and back home. Remi and I head for the room while Gus gets ready for work. She places her SpacePad face-up on her bed and plays her stupid synth-pop beside a holographic LED fixture of lights. But that's her side of the room—and I never care to hear that shit. So, I go into our bathroom to change into my spaceship and moonlight pajama pants and hear Gus enter our room as the bidet splashes over his words. And while lotioning my shins, water flushes over Remi's response.

I enter our room, and Gus has both arms locked behind his back, asking, "What's the point of seeing him if you can't bring him here?"

"I don't know," says Remi. "We're still getting to know each other."

"Turn this mess down. Tell me, where and when are you seeing him?"

"His work, and we ride the same train—."

"You aren't skipping school? Are you?"

"No. I'm not."

"Watch your tone, little lady."

"We didn't even know about Shauren until last night."

"That's completely different," Gus responds. "Young Avantians are all born just waiting for the silver spoon like goldfish in a pond."

"What…" she says, spiking out her fingers. "He's mature for his age."

"How old?"

"Do we have to do this, now? Don't you have work?"

Gus leaves the apartment. Remi gets up from her bed and heads for the bathroom. She returns with a caked-over facial and lightened eyebrows, grabbing crochet tops from the closet. "Where's my black-hooded jacket?" she asks, spreading each top across her bed.

"You're leaving?" I ask as she rummages through my side

of our closet. "I don't keep up with your stuff."

"Ugh… Move," she says, crumpling her fingers.

"Nothing over here is yours."

"…freakin' hate this place."

"Where are you going?"

"Could it be any more obvious? People who have friends actually go out on Fridays."

Remi storms into the kitchen and fills a cup of ice water, and our front door sounds off. It's Gus, walking in through the living room, mumbling, "Hat. Badge. Hat. Badge." He rushes into his bedroom, yelling, "I'm going to be late over this—" Silent and still, Remi remains in the kitchen while Gus peeks into our room. "Where is she?" he asks.

"Laundry."

He looks at his wrist, "*Abeg*," and rushes out the front door.

Remi storms back into our room and shuts the window blinds. She struts across in a panic, leaving wakes of perfume and powder seeping across my bed.

"You're welcome?" I suggest.

"For why?"

"I could've said kitchen."

"Good thing he's running late."

"Or that he didn't go into the kitchen looking for his watch?"

"And where's my black-hooded jacket?"

"Is it in the kitchen?"

"Really?" she says, balling her fist. "Until tonight, I thought he just worked and came back here. Does it even cross your mind he's out there enjoying life with a rich white woman? While we're just—"

"How do you know she's rich?"

"You left me alone with that lady at the restaurant."

"You could've left, too."

"Do you think before you talk?" Remi asks.

"Yeah. Like when I didn't say 'kitchen'…"

"Say 'kitchen' one more—"

"I don't think your jacket is in the kitchen; I think it's in the hallway nook."

"Did you move it?"

"No. I said I think—so…"

She grabs her jacket, rushes to the living room, and pulls out her L.D.S. to connect to her SpaceTalk. "Rigil," she shouts. "I'm leaving. Keep this door and your mouth shut."

V.3

On Monday, this girl, she stares from my eight o'clock. [That's behind me to the left] It's in class, so there's nowhere to go. And nowhere to run. I could jump out the window. But that would hurt. It would also be loud.

And so, I don't do that.

I place my phone face down, set both elbows above my desk, and twirl my pen just like McCall does when he can't handle the pressure of a kid on the spectrum staring directly into his eyes. I bow my head between my left shoulder pit where I can watch the girl thumb through her phone, look at me, and then back to her phone.

Mahan, my guts, configures this 'what if' data by responding with waves of hope and lust crashing up my vagus nerve. I fight it like a foreign entity penetrating my stomach and preparing me for an ill-advised battle with the devil's oar—soluting his soldiers to full mast.

"Excuse me, Mrs. Panegry." Maurice, the school's athletic trainer, pokes his head through the classroom doorway. "Sorry to disturb you all, but I need to take Rigil for a few moments." I get the go-ahead from Mrs. Panegry, grab my ViDi notepad, and slide out from the desk, holding the notepad over my waist area.

"You can leave your stuff," Maurice suggests. "We won't be long."

…but he must understand.

He pulls out a slice of gum and breaks it down with his teeth like a bony fillet of catfish. "Do you have plans for the holiday break?" he asks, stepping into the orange-walled hallway.

"I'll be playing basketball and sleeping."

"Sleep is for the weak. But I'll need your speed and your toughness."

"Track?"

"No. Football," he says. "I see something more in you. Can you come out for weight conditioning with us in December?"

"I'll still have basketball."

"Banks, am I wasting my time?"

"Wouldn't conditioning get in the way of basketball?"

Maurice leans his back against the hallway wall and crosses his legs. "Listen," he says, holding the gum at the side of his left cheek. "This morning, at the grocery store, I was scooping dried cranberries out of the bulk bin for my kale salad, okay? When I dumped my last scoop into the bag, I noticed a handful was spilling onto the floor beside the bin. When I got to the checkout counter, guess what?"

"...spilled cranberries were waiting for you?"

"No," he laughs. "They charged me for the cranberries I spilled."

"So?"

"Do you think I paid for the mess I made?"

"Shrugs."

"Would you have paid?" he asks.

Shifting gears back at my desk, the conversation with

Maurice attracts another pair of eyes—this time detected at my three o'clock.

She turns.

She stares.

She muses,

And I…drop my yellow highlighter marker.

It rolls down to a step where I can't grab it—yet—because it's Monday, and she's giving me one more thing to readjust this early in the week. I crouch below my desk, stretching my foot toward the marker to scoot it to the left, and…I see my eight o'clock who still observes.

"Rigil," says Mrs. Panegry. "You must be popular today. This gentleman is here to speak with you as well."

He stands at the classroom doorway in ankle-cut jeans above strapless matching suede loafers. I'll say his hair is strawberry blonde, hanging to the shoulders of his true-blue blazer holding rose-gold cuffed links at the sleeve. I follow the gentleman out to the halls, where he places his left hand into his pocket and walks further down the hallway to the gradient end, where the walls turn blue. He leans against the sky-blue paint, crossing his legs and settling both hands in his pockets. His chin elevates like Big Men did when scouting TheValleys. "You like this place?" he asks.

"School?"

"I figured you didn't. So, your parent or guardian is…"

"Are you asking about Gus?"

"Yes. Yusmata?"

"No one says that to him."

"…ain't so Slick after all?" he mumbles. "What is he to you?"

"He's…Is he okay?"

"Yeah," he smiles. "I spoke with him just before coming to see you."

"He was awake?"

"How else would he be putting food on the table tonight?"

Between us and our dilated pupils is my racing heart, massaging the layers of my chest. But it's the white noise of TheDistrict's crème de la crème dressed Ambassador who breathes an echo of no words, no description—like the invisible baggage we forever chuck over our backs every morning we wake up. "Who are you?" I ask.

"I'm with DDSD," he says. "District Defense and Segregations Department. And Remilee, she's your sister?"

"But what's your purpose?"

"My purpose? Are you taking up sports?"

"Excuse me, sir," shouts Maurice from down the hall. "Do you have a visitor's badge?"

The gentleman whispers, "Must be a coach the way he's chewing that damn gum like that. Hello, how are you?"

"Name, please?" Maurice asks.

"Mr. Jefferies, Leonard Jefferies." He extends his hand to Maurice, who stares at it, looks at me, and scratches his ears as though he heard him—but it's *fuck you* for now, okay? "I'm an old friend of his father's," says Jefferies. "Just seeing how his two are doing. But I couldn't find Remilee in her classroom."

"Are you familiar with this guy?" Maurice asks, pointing his thumb at Jefferies.

"Oh, it's been so long," says Jefferies. "And they've gone through so much since moving here. Gosh, you've gotten tall."

"Sir, your badge," says Maurice.

Jefferies searches across his pockets and chest as though someone stole it. "Must've left it on top of the sign-in desk downstairs," he claims. "But hey, I've got a two o'clock. We're surprising Gus for his birthday tomorrow afternoon at work, so don't spoil it," he winks.

In a conniving walk toward the staircase, Jefferies puts both hands back into his pockets, turns around, and winks at the both of us, twice. He whistles like the calve who couldn't tie his shoes, calculating each step down to the first floor, leaving a merit of welcome to his world of lost shoelaces.

Maurice spits his gum into the trash can, "Banks," he says. "Our practice field…it won't be as green as the kale salad

I ate for lunch today."

V.4

Summer starts in June...because we've always paid attention to the duration of the brightest full Strawberry MOON when the days are longest and many nights are warmer.

...yet slower because on Mondays, in football, we practice team oneness. We run the Potomac Overlook, led by coach Maurice—who ensures the fat boys don't make it to the top first. Tuesdays, he reinforces team stillness, where those with ADHD feel the [business] through a pair of Chinese meditation balls. Wednesdays, we journal, "I WANNA WIN, AND I WANNA WIN NOW," for thirty minutes. On Thursdays and Fridays, we prepare for July.

.

.

.

...when we practice under the peak of the SUN, the pinnacle of heat, humidity, and beyond muscle cramps and chest burns. Coach Maurice... he's curious to see who can jump rope the longest or until a lineman's calve curls up beside their shins like a slice of bacon shriveling on a hot nonstick pan. Coach Maurice... he's curious to see which receiver faints or vomits first during knee highs. And by all means of pain and angst, Coach Maurice, he helps us create our room, our space, but responsibly—because he understands there needs to be an on/off switch.

From our red rooms of… we pad up in the name of safety, sprinting until seeing black—and bear-crawling until our inner caged dogs get to huffing and puffing across the practice fields. By the end of practice, the field is painted red from the blood of exhaustion and rashes of grit. By the end of practice, the only thing holding our tackle sleds together are the slices of gum Coach Maurice spat.

August, I fly back to the hardwood battlefield. And once again, ascending toward the highest cirrus clouds, looking down from my window seat and confirming earth's curve. The trip out west with McCall's basketball club is my first flight since arriving in the TheDistrict—when the chambers of Mahan, my imagination factory, open its gates to manifest my ingenious spaceship. A place in mind, at heart, and somewhere behind my eyes that allows me to voyage between the piers of our noosphere. I recall the viewing porch of Pier III and its white noise—scathing, soaring, and canvassing the comfort of thought by how it docked upon my port with an aggressive 'bang' down my ear canal as the aircraft descended. I peeked out the window to get a bird's eye view of the Avantian Motherboard for the first time as it spread like moss—yet

BUDD HANSEN

vibrant and calm. But upon another descent, today, I see how land below is still sectioned off by squares—a view exposing how farmers are the only Avantians abstracting TheDistrict's true borders of separation.

◆

After deboarding our flight from the tournament, Gus and Shauren meet me at the arrival's platform. On a long walk to the car, Shauren reaches for Gus, yearning for kisses while toggling his fingers for a handhold.

Gus winces each time.

But with a third try, she gets what she wants.

And then it's me, climbing into her back seat as if I'm the virus en route—waiting to be circulated through the plastered chips of TheDistrict's circuit board.

We merge onto the D-I-95 SuperChannel, and Shauren's poking at Gus, again, begging for... He turns around, stares me in the eye, and glances out the rear window with his portrait-esque face. "What?" I ask.

He faces forward, asking, "How was the tournament?"

"Fine. We lost some and won some." We then pass our Lone Avenue exit. "Can you take me to the apartment?" I ask.

Shauren exhales. Gus scratches his head. "No," he responds. "We don't live there anymore."

"Where do we live now?"

Shauren, again, takes a deep breath and shakes her head.

"Can't believe you waited this long," she mutters.

"A lot happened over the weekend," says Gus. "We decided to move in together. Which means you finally get your own room."

"Did you get a bigger place?"

"I still have the loft at Dekum Court," says Shauren. She then pokes Gus, pleading, "Can you speak up?"

"How am I getting my own room?" I ask.

"Remi, she's moving out next weekend," Gus responds. "And with her boy… friend—who we still haven't met. Do you understand this guy?"

"No. So you moved my stuff?"

"Yep. Everything's in boxes for you to unpack when we get to her place," he says.

I trace the door's thermal detector with my index finger, and its airflow blows back across my pores, drying the leaking waters of Mahan. Shauren glances at Gus, but he immediately faces forward, raising his eyebrows through her moonroof. She glimpses back at me, "Are you going to be okay?" she asks.

"Shrugs."

"The good news is," Shauren says, pausing to smile. "I'm getting a bigger place this spring. I figured we'd wait until after both football and basketball season to make the bigger move." I feel Shauren looking back through her rearview mirror as I gaze outside her car's window at the browning grass of Dekum Station's transit center. We pass a row of cookie-cutter rowhouses with slanted rooftops and solar panels next to their mid-level staircases. The windows of each unit are uniquely placed—some big enough to be the side panel wall while other windows wrap around an entire floor. "This is your new neighborhood," she says. We turn into her building's parkade and drive one level lower to her unit's garage quarters. "Doesn't sound like he's happy," she whispers.

"He'll be fine," says Gus. "He's just hard to read."

"I guess I can help with your backpack," says Shauren, glaring up at Gus. He climbs out of her car and walks right to her lower-level garage exit with just himself, doubling up the steps with only his palms by his side.

My duffle weighs heavier with each step toward Shauren's door. And here I am, here I stand, grounded by gravity's best characteristic in my new home, for now. Her ceiling's vaulted, the floor is marble, and I figure it's heated because Gus already has his shoes and socks off.

While cardboard boxes reek of an empty soul menacing across my new bedroom, a dusting odor reaches my nostrils with the fumes of a cleansed dead body.

Who did they torture?

My bedroom's vaulted ceiling looks down upon Earth's wobble, echoing every footstep as I tip-toe to shut the door. I open my window, and the birds don't sing. Why would they chirp this late anyway? It's a rural neighborhood—quiet and modest as the cars drive silently against the concrete paved back streets. So, why would they chant if the cars aren't roaring?

But the ringing in my ears and this carpet turning to mire, or smudge, like a wetland's paradise molding—contaminates the hardwood floors rotting from the hallway. If the water's running hot, they've muted its cooperation with oxygen. Here's a box, there's a box. Must I become one to fit in? Or live inside one to stay out? I figure this is where white noise becomes—

I lie face down on Shauren's carbon-infused pillow top mattress to watch my thoughts run off the Richter. A scale on which conscious vibrancy becomes memories, floating through bliss, sort of like dust. And as my fingers turn to forks, I poke at the memories, serving myself a late-night entree of recollections with a side of premonition. But how they're presented is unperceivable and out of order, much like dust.

…now, residing on the other side of the imagination factory, Gus and Shauren see me off to TheDistrict's juvenile psych ward across the street from the Library's Amphitheatre—where I spend my days writing my name on the red wall so I don't forget who they're calling when it's time for mushy peas and a broiled Salisbury steak. And after what's weaved through the hallways of Joe' Prep's grapevine, embarrassment would determine my hermit lifestyle—slim, rogue, and recluse.

…a bit like dust.

This is forever known about me because the grapevines of hearsay ain't so sweet.

…the mind is what *they* torture.

V.5

"Rigil…" it's the concern in Shauren's voice as she rushes through the bedroom door. "Are you okay?" She places her hands beneath my head, and a blurring Gus stands in the doorway.

"What happened?" he asks.

"Please," Shauren urges. "Just help me get him off the floor."

Gus grabs my feet as Shauren lifts me by the back of my head. "Did you fall?" he asks.

"How would he—"

"He's probably jet-lagged," says Gus.

"You're kidding?"

"What?"

"Look at your son. His skin is pale, and his shirt is soaked."

"Keep going; tell me more about my son."

"You're being an insensitive prick," says Shauren. "This isn't normal."

"So, he got lightheaded."

"Huh?"

"His blood sugar is probably low," Gus assumes.

"He just had a freakin' panic attack."

"How do you know?"

"Does it cross your mind how long I've been working with teenagers?"

"Okay…can you not talk to me like one?"

"This isn't about you, Gus. Look at his eyes. And he hasn't even said anything. Is he anemic? What's his blood pressure like? You gotta know these things."

"Stop it."

"This is your son."

"He gets physicals through the athletic department. He's been fine."

"That just means he can dribble a damn ball and knock a kid to the ground."

"So, that's all I've been paying for?"

"My gosh…I can't," says Shauren. "Will you focus on

your son while I get him water?"

I'm left with the smirk on his face, the Jack Slick on his sleeves, and the man who feels no comfort. He conceals the bearing of her disapproving face—a man who only speaks tough love through his shapeshifting grit. "Shauren's very concerned for you," Gus whispers, thumbing my forehead. "But I can tell you're getting close to yourself. Sleep will be very important from here on, okay?"

Shauren rushes back in and hugs my head. She lifts me from my nape and pours water down my throat. And for Mr. Slick, he leaves the room by the scold of her eyes.

"Oh boy, what an evening," says Gus, yawning and stretching through the hallway. "And it's my night off."

"...still just all about you, isn't it?" Shauren shouts. Her pupils become whiter than the sheets I've yet to tuck onto my mattress. She then caresses my chest, causing those things we call goosebumps to rise and spread because, don't you remember...? I am the virus. I am... "It's okay if football and basketball are too much for you," she says. "I'll leave a message with Dr. Brody; she has her own practice. I really think we should go and see her this week."

Gus pokes his head through the doorway. "Isn't she just a school counselor?" he asks.

"No," says Shauren. "She's also a naturopath. Didn't I tell you about her new district contract last year?"

"Abeg," he gasps. "I wouldn't think to call her this late."

"Again, she and I have been doing this together for a very long time."

"So, she's like family?" he asks.

"No. Dr. Brody is nothing like them."

◆

They reside in the community of Grossmont, where a diverse cluster of houses showcases the past bidding wars of architectural monopoly. The only incentive for TheDistrict to see this neighborhood thrive is the luxury tax that property owners pay to have the freedom to be creative about constructing their homes—making the community a hidden gem for tourists outside of the Bourgeoisie Tower at Saint Laurent'co Circle. The schools would've gone bankrupt had they all been private; however, with the historic parks in the area, the multi-family homes set a standard for various developmental possibilities. That is, homes with white picket fences or brick pillar gates protecting their long driveways next to front lawns wrapping around to their backyards. Every other lawn is brown, making the neighborhood look like a multicultural checkered board from a bird's eye view. Some houses look like contemporary boxes painted by the local preschool, while others are built to look like an empress's palace, surrounded by a moat filled with tears of joy. Their modern-day igloos are ugly, but they're gaining popularity amongst a young minimalist group of wealthy Nordic descendants.

And then there are houses like Aunt Maurrie's, Shauren's sister's, who lives in a newly built Georgian with a Cape Cod barn out back. Both were constructed on an acre and a half of clay. Her brown and beige estate sits on one of the largest lots in the area. But the house sucks…

It's where I acquire the tradition of giving thanks by showing up to experience *their* lessons through ignorance—and accept a collaborative practice where hors d'oeuvres are set across a cherrywood tabletop, and later, we overeat dry turkey.

…scorned if absent.

I'm talking about autumn's last holiday, gathering around cousins and extended uncles in the white-walled living room bordered with beige drapes. Her granite and mirror-paneled bar counter shelves the liquor glasses where those who need to be drunk around family, shoot the shit and circle the boxes. Her theater occupies a room full of sports heads, seated in a staggering row of plush leather seats where they yell at the projector screen, suggesting what football play should be next—yet none of their jaws have ever experienced the resistance of an over-chewed stick of gum.

Kids congregate in the basement next to her late husband's fully functional workshop—which leads to their lower-level garage, where the younger adults smoke numbers and pin tales on rogue donkeys. I spot the two familial black sheep making their way through each generation and eventually finding a corner to soak up until everyone's eaten so they can make a to-go plate and leave without a courteous round of goodbyes.

As conversations weave from kitchen island countertops to a memoir-filled dining room, Gus doubles down on the cranberry sauce and smothers gravy across his marble porcelain plate. He's first to his seat, waiting, circling his thumbs as though it's too soon and eager of him to be such a famished looking guest. But he protects the two open seats by his side as the Penners fill their plates around Aunt Maurrie's extended rustic dining table. The cousin—he waits, looking into the ether of space from the end of the table. He paces his eyes between sips of wine from a medallion glass—scanning left to right.

But he's not mysterious.

He's an autty who'll only be questioned...

Aunt Maurrie grabs his wine, pours it into a thicker glass, and hands it back to him. "Rigil, are you enjoying Joseph Prep?" she asks, placing the medallion glass on a napkin. "Did Shauren tell you we've got some long-lost kinfolk working there?"

"Sis," says Shauren.

"It's cool," I shrug.

"Does Dayton play in your conference?" Maurrie asks.

Shauren responds, "Dayton's a private institute out here. Our clubs would only scrimmage them."

"They must've changed that after the strikes?" Maurrie assumes. "Who did you all scrimmage in football?"

"I didn't play this year."

"You didn't? What happened?"

"Sis, the boy's hungry," says Shauren.

"At least employees are coming from the same neighboring areas."

"What are you talking about?" Shauren asks.

"Isn't that how you met Gus?"

"She's talking about the job fair," says Gus, placing his hand on Shauren's left leg. Yet he blushes a black rose blooming from his cheek, smiling, "And it all started on my first day in Uptown," he says.

"What?" I ask.

"The Ambassador at the 'W' Bank," he responds.

Shauren retracts her head by the neck, "...thought you said you just showed up to apply?"

"*Probably because he lied.*"

"That's how you found out about the job fair?" Shauren asks.

"The Ambassador referred me," says Gus. "She came

right up to us. Ahli, you remember?" His grimace folds the table, shortening its length because Shauren has spotted the frog in his throat as she pierces down his tonsils. "I don't like that look," Gus stutters.

"You don't just meet an Ambassador fresh off an airplane from TrenchPort and never tell your partner," says Shauren.

Gus wipes gravy off his lips, leaving chapped skin crust on his embroidered linen napkin. The moment is saved, however, as the front door opens and Shauren grabs Gus to excuse themselves from the table. "Remilee, my little lady," Gus praises through the foyer.

Maurrie excuses herself next, leaving an eternity of calm across the table between me and the *cousin* who's figured it out but can never explain it to his family. Shauren's voice progresses through the hallway with Remi, who enters first, wearing a black jumpsuit and matching water-resistant boots. And speaking with his swaying, Slick hands, Gus ushers the boy into the dining room, explaining the food table against the wall as though he prepped it.

The boy catches me sipping my lemon water, so I look away, put it down, and gently grab it again to take another sip. He gleams directly at me—maybe taken a liking to my refreshing lemon water? But then it's Remi—she pauses, asking, "…you two know each other?"

JOURNAL VI

High School Daze (cont'd)

"WE MADE FRIED CHICKEN FOR you all," Maurrie announces, carrying a linen basket of battered fried poultry from her kitchen. Remi's boyfriend rolls his eyes and sits next to Gus, who sniffs the steaming basket of meat hard enough that you'd think cocaine is burning off the batter.

Remi takes the seat between the men of her life and pours them both a glass of lemon water from the stainless-steel pitcher. The boy sips, stares, pondering to ask, "Wait a minute, who are you?"

"Astrist," Remi points. "This is Rigil Ahli, my younger brother."

"Did you work at that coffee shop on Lone Avenue?" I ask.

Astrist's eyes brighten, "Yeah," he says. "I thought you

looked familiar."

"You've been there?" Remi asks.

"Small world, isn't it?" says Gus. "You could set his room on fire, and he'd—"

"Do you still work there?" I ask.

My question flies over Astrist's head—seemingly distracted by the antics of our drunken father and Remi, his coddling girlfriend. Although she's my sister, a new woman blooms within the vicinities of her baristo. Her eyes, much vibrant, radiant, and glowing—as she moves with purpose to attend to Astrist's plate setting. You'd think she grew up having idolized a nuptial model. But no. The women she respected, she feared because they dressed in Vanta.

"When were you at The Bean Palace?" Remi asks.

"Last year, when he kicked me out of the apartment with those almonds he stole from church." Gus leans back in an outburst of laughter, slapping his right leg so hard that his kneecap pops through his skin and falls on Maurrie's Persian carpet.

Astrist turns to Remi, saying, "Remember, I told you I once met a young dude from TrenchPort?"

"But you said his father was in real estate."

"That's what he told me."

Shauren interjects, "Gus barely tells me what he's doing Uptown in that black building."

"But it's Astrist, though?" Gus asks.

"Though, what?" he responds.

"…making sure I speak your name correctly," says Gus. "And how do you like working over there?"

Astrist exhales, "It's good for now. My mom's selling the lease to Rollin' Noodles."

"Oh wow," says Gus. "She owns the place? Is she retiring?"

"No. She used to work for the GTube's rail union."

"Was she an admin?" Gus asks.

"She was recruited to program the railway's fail-safe systems—like when people or things get stuck across the tracks. It was basically a suicide prevention project."

"Well, that's interesting," says Shauren.

"But she got tired of all the drudge work after they made it political," says Astrist. "And that's what started The Bean Palace."

Gus twirls his thumbs in admiration, withholding his tiptoeing responses at the edge of his tongue. He gazes into Astrist's eyes and watches the boy speak in amazement—as though each word flies off his tongue. But they're taking off sort of how Dumbo did when he first had trouble believing he could fly.

…he carries a sunburnt stutter.

"His family is like venture capitalists," says Remi.

"That's not what we do," Astrist clarifies.

"But you said you guys capitalize on new adventures."

With half the family stuffed with dry turkey and watered-down gravy, country music blasts out of an eight-piece surround sound system from the living room theatre. Aubrey, the uncle, commences his lone two-step get-down, inviting Gus to a dual left-foot dance-off. Another aunt takes her glutted belly toward the two-man drunken hoedown, where a drunken Gus grabs her left hand. And off each of his opening feet, he triple-steps a sway, swings her out, and spins her back into his arms. He tries whipping her back up from an over-swaying dip but staggers into a standing speaker and knocks it to the ground.

"Hey, hey, watch it," Aunt Maurrie screams, rushing over in a panic.

"Sorry," says Gus. "It's like dancing with two trying to swing her out."

"You imbecile!" Maurrie shouts.

She glares.

She pauses.

…she smacks her right palm across Gus's left cheek—turning his face toward Remi and Astrist to where he's stuck, facing them for long enough that I could write an essay on how *he could never*.

"What was that for?" Shauren asks, standing at the dining room table.

Maurrie strikes her index finger against Gus's nose, taunting, "Don't you dare talk about our sis' like that."

Gus pleads with forgiving hands, "Was it something I said?"

And so, we go home, where Shauren places our to-go containers across the kitchen countertop because we weren't done eating. Gus comes out of the bathroom, opens one container, and picks at the food with his bare hands. "Seriously," says Shauren. "I didn't hear the water running. Please." She smacks his hand and slides hand sanitizer across the counter.

Gus exits the kitchen and pulls his sweater off through the hallway. He leaves it on the dusted floor for Shauren as she gasps aggressively to pick it up and follows him into the bedroom. Shauren stomps through the hallway, and I hear him, PLUNK—Gus goes stomach first onto the bed. "Get up and brush your teeth," she says. "You snored all the drive here, and now my car smells like red wine and turkey-shit." Minutes later, Gus paces through the hall, brushing his teeth, "Really, dude…" says Shauren. "You do this in the morning, too."

"You just told me to brush my——."

"Stop. You're getting it all over the floors."

"What now?" says Gus.

"Ugh. It's like you tour the entire apartment to do this, dripping toothpaste drool all over my floors and carpet."

"I'll clean it up."

"No, you won't. Just go back in there," Shauren says, pressing a roll of paper towels against his chest. She proceeds to shove him toward the bathroom until their room door slams.

Their voices percolate through the hallway and drywall, having an adverse effect on my ability to peacefully enjoy my Thursday evening recording of *funny news*. The type of news that brings humor at a time of war. And the kind of show that makes light of hell, especially when thinking you should care but realize you're not the only one who can't give a rat's flying buttocks about... These shows make me feel in tune with others who breathe the breaths of aloof.

I doze off but awaken to their room door opening as Gus snatches his jacket and boots from the hallway closet. "Are you leaving?" I ask.

"I'll be back," he says, shutting the door.

I rest my head north toward her window to face west, where the TV screen is bright enough because otherwise, it's dark—and I must be able to see if Shauren has monsters beneath her couch that she hasn't told us about.

But Shauren storms out of the room, asking, "Did he leave?"

"Looked like it."

"Why does your father get so defensive?"

"What did he say?"

"To me? Or my sister?"

"The pregnant one?" I ask.

"Dude, you guys," Shauren says, walking back to her room and slamming the door.

We're misunderstood.

Much how a kid in a SpaceLook group quotes me telling a referee, 'Live in my village, your throat is white meat.'

VI.2

Midseason, sophomore year, we're at Blotsburg High. All game, I'm catching elbows by the kid running point. He cuts hard to the basket, smirking sharp enough to know it's mixed with baking soda on the weekends—yet evident that the summer basketball circuit keeps him out of trouble during off-season. Throughout the fourth quarter, he gets away with three striking elbows into my spleen. And each time, the ref looks away.

Consequently, I get really, really mad.

After his last elbow, my backhand pauses midway through slapping the whistle out of the ref's mouth for chewing it. But then he blows it—holding out both index fingers in the form of a 'T.'

So, I run to center court and slap the air there.

Dust apparently hits back as I'm scratching my eyelids, rubbing my throat, and coughing up a lung while walking off the court. I cover my mouth only to hear a small section of students mocking me as they rub their eyes, booing and hooting as if I'm crying.

McCall throws his SpacePad onto his chair, but it ricochets off and falls to the floor, shattering his screen. Security guards rush toward McCall as the floor sweepers try cleaning up the broken glass, but the mess is scattered by teammates and assistant coaches. Eventually, they're able to direct our rage down to our locker room.

The bus drops us off outside the Joe' Prep gymnasium, and I walk three blocks for a GTube heading into SouthStation, where I find the most glistening tile of track one's platform to stare through. I stand above a buffered surface and watch the girl in my peripheral at the charging station paint the river bends of the Potomac's calming flow. She switches to pencils and sketches a mountain range in the background. But what appears to be three moons rising over the horizon tells me she's of us, *Children of the Sphere*, projecting her most inner known lands of clover berries and coconut milk—where adults find ways to keep raindrops in their back pockets.

I let a train go by, now sunken into the most heart-thumping trough, musing across track two, trying to decipher if the girl's river is actually the Panaya. I take a second look, and she's colored in the clouds, leaving two moons but now a bison at the summit. I walk closer and see that her clouds are smoke off the security guard's cigarette lingering from behind her.

With six minutes until another arrival, I grab my phone, and the loudest heartbeat pounces across the tracks in response to 99-plus notifications I shouldn't be seeing.

I peruse my SpaceFeed and find the outrage of my actions on the court having spawned a SpaceLook group by the Blotsburg students called, 'FUCK YOU, RIGIL!!! (*you should be suspended*)'.

I board and notice more people riding than expected, including an elderly lady sitting in the back. Before riding beneath the Potomac, where it gets dark, I look her in the eye, assuring her I'm one of the good ones.

With four metro stops to go—again, my heart does the jumping jacks to 31 inbox messages, all in bold; however, the most daring is from a Vinetra Longwood.

"AHLIKO, HOW ARE YOU?? WE JUST WATCHED YOU ON PADN SPORTS CAST. HAD NO IDEA YOUR FAMILY MOVED HERE! HOW IS REMI? IS SHE STILL SINGING SONGS FROM 'UNTOUCHABLE'? ...YOUR CURIOSITY MUST'VE LED YOU TO A BASKETBALL COURT?"

This moment, that message, couldn't be any more random.

Dekum Station's transit center has a treacherous staircase, where the top step takes me to the corner of the block—where I stand two blocks from Shauren's corner-wrapping window that dims through her living room blinds.

I approach her bottom step, and she opens the door. "You're back late," she says. "Is everything okay?"

"Did Dr. Brody call you?"

"No, but I know your bus dropped you off well over an hour ago."

"I missed the train."

"It's not even a 30-minute ride from the school. Why the attitude?" she asks, following me through the hallway. "You know who told me about your ejection?" I continue walking, setting my duffle bag down because my breath feels short and my tide's running high. "I can't believe this," she says. "At least do me a favor and tell me who Leonard Jefferies is."

Shauren shows me her brightened phone screen, displaying a text conversation from a phone number and area code foreign to Capitol Parish. "Now I got your attention?"

"Isn't he a friend of Gus?"

"Then why hasn't he responded to my text? This, 'Mr. Jefferies' guy, said he was at your game and watched you throw a temper tantrum all over the court."

"No… just the center." Yet still, my heartbeat sinks into the lowest trough—faster and lower than it raced across the train tracks.

"Do you know him?" she asks. "I didn't think you guys knew anyone like that."

"Like what?"

VI.3

Before the final home game of my sophomore season, McCall cancels Thursday's practice, freeing up the evening for a rare moment where Gus and I speak.

…and a rare view of evening daylight, burning through Shauren's corridor as the sunsets later this time of year. She works out of her office nook, where her walls are filled with certificates, licenses, and credentials that document her permission to provide such news and information to her SpaceFeed viewers. Lecturing teachers through SpaceTalk is her way of supervising their tactics and harnessing some spite of which she can't get through with Gus. Her work may be fine, but relationships are fickle. At best, some part conniving.

And so, here's Gus, stretching and yawning through the halls. "Ahliko, boy, come," he shouts from the kitchen. He stands at the kitchen counter, chewing leftover shrimp and salmon bites, glaring lustfully out the living room window. "Do you hear this?" he asks. Buzzing car tires ripping the pavement, kids laughing at the corners coming home from school, and our SUN breaking through Shauren's skylight above—providing an evening of candor white noise with him as he pushes the plate of food across the counter, asking, "Do you want some?"

"I'll eat what Shauren cooks later."

"She cleaned your bathroom and wants to know why lotion was next to the toilet."

"It's where I moisturize after the shower."

"You sure?"

"Yes."

"Well, she wasn't," says Gus. "But she wants you to do your laundry from now on."

"Hey, Rigil," says Shauren, coming from her office. "Did he tell you when he's leaving?"

"Where are you going?" I ask.

Gus flickers his eyes, turning away from Shauren, "Iceland," he says. "We got a supplier up there, and my team is supporting the plant's implementation."

Shauren grazes his shoulder, asking, "And, meeting old friends up there?"

"Leonard?" I ask.

"No, Nwaka," says Shauren.

"Who did you say?" Gus asks.

"Wait," says Shauren. "You do know a Leonard Jeff— He better not be who I think he is." Gus devours the biggest salmon bite, separates the shrimp tails, and chugs his water. "He was at the game a few weeks ago," she says.

"Why…" Gus grunts.

"I didn't see him," I respond. "But he texted Shauren."

"Why didn't you tell me?" he asks.

"Whoa. Easy," says Shauren. "My gosh. I told you that night."

"You couldn't tell me this yourself?" he asks.

"He didn't say anything to me," I respond.

Gus crosses his arms, leans back, and swallows, asking, "So you've never spoken to him?"

"…no."

"Gus…" says Shauren. "What's this about? Can you talk? Is this how you communicate?"

Gus flexes his nose. His eyes fade black. And lips fold inward. Yet polite enough to wash his plate and trash his shrimp shells—leaving Shauren to watch, glare, and bask in contempt. "I've got packing to do," Gus whispers, leaving the kitchen.

◆
◆
◆

A week passed our full Snow MOON—it's early March—and warm enough to run to our final home game against Blotsburg, tipping off at seven o'clock. I trot my first mile across the park blocks of Capitol Parish, kicking up brown grass and weaving between trees of which can only breathe my name. I run my second mile and pass the black rose gardens of Dekum Station's transit center. And through my third mile, I ease across an overpass to bask in the views of the city's rising apples, expanding oranges, and bright sky-stabbing bananas. I sprint the last mile before the gymnasium, which inevitably primes me for the mayhem across the wooden battlefield—

...where the bleachers fill with our diverse student body, eager to cheer us on through every play. How our punk rock frat boys walk in seemingly on time, pounding fists with the preps and slapping hands with the jocks, it's a shallow work of social art at its finest. Holistically, they aren't friends—they only interact when there's a group project in class. One section of the bleachers is the standing degenerates—pounding the floor, vibrating the soles of my firmly strapped sneakers. They shout and chant, causing my palms to dampen the leather coverings of the game ball during warmups. Some girls care too much to look cute, smelling deathly perfumed over us sweaty teenage boys playing for either respect or a decent future. Our Uptown-dressed posh girls are scolded by the parents and teachers—who attend these games to support their child or student because it's odd if a parent can make it to a game, and doesn't…

Fifteen minutes into warmups, the officials tell McCall and me that the Blotsburg point guard has been pre-warned about temperament. And advises us that any overtly frustrating antics won't be tolerated.

Just before the game-ending buzzer, Tokaiya dribbles out the clock and crosses half-court. At the two-second mark, he picks up his dribble, sets the ball on the court, and rolls it toward the feet of the Blotsburg point guard. Facing away from the ball, I anticipate the buzzer as I walk to our bench.

"Skunk, bitches," someone yells as the whistle blows.

McCall throws his arms in the air, and the ball is chucked at our basket. Unaware of who'd thrown the ball or shouted those words, 0.4 seconds remain, and the refs continue their huddling discussion. Security rolls out their sectional dividers to keep students from pouring onto the court. Two groups from the top of each bleacher stand, begin shouting back and forth, chanting as the refs close out a 45-second standstill of non-play.

The game is called, and we're directed toward the roped-off section between the locker room entrance and the gymnasium's rear exit. Tokaiya walks behind me between two security guards, passing by a crowd of kids leaving the visiting student section.

Tokaiya stops as his jersey is yanked and snatched by a boy jumping the rope and swinging but merely scrapes Tokaiya's face. Another fist emerges from the crowd but is caught by the lone fending security guard beside us. Students rush toward the commotion as more fists and arms are thrown through the chaos. One kid running directly at me pulls down his hoodie and cocks his arm long enough that I grab and twist his fist. Then he slips—only for three other Blotsburg jersey-wearing kids to jump the rope and trample the poor boy.

The security guard tries pulling off one of the boys, but the boy loses his balance and plummets to the floor. Tokaiya smashes that boy's face with the bottom of his sneakers—bringing two other kids to jump past security and onto my back because I was next to join. Our teammates try rushing past P.A.P.D. officers, but they're held back at the locker room doorway. Tokaiya remains wrestling on the floor with the same kid, while the boy who swung first gets tugged off my back and dragged to the hardwood floor as I'm brought down with him.

Now, his back faces me.

…so I pound through his spine with my fist.

I do it again.

And again—

…right below his rear rib cage.

"Yeah, he'll feel that knuckle-sandwich in the morning."

A large male security guard grabs me around my waist and carries me out of the gymnasium's rear emergency exit, shouting, "Chill out, young man."

Fuck that.

"Me, MAD…"

VI.4

Gazing at our three brightest bulbs of midnight, the nearest MOON projects my name loudest, "Rigil Ahli, Rigil Ahli," and the ground trembles, rumbling my inner-known lands of silk and berries. "Rigil Ahli, Rigil Ahli," the voice repeats. The furthest MOON fades with night, and the middle is predicted to follow. I widen my oval-eye view of the skies, but it's Shauren, nudging me in the chest. She wakes me out of a deep novel venture through Mahan's path—a place I can only dream of seeing at the awakening hours—a place, for now, I can only see behind my eyelids. "Were you having a bad dream?" she asks. "Here, sip your water." The first gulp spills and soaks my pillow.

"What's that look for?" I ask.

"...sounded like a nightmare," she says.

"I was dreaming."

"Same difference."

"Not if it's where I'd rather be. Is there some concern? Your face is..."

"We should get you checked for sleep apnea," she says. "You're twitching, talking, and—"

"Sleeping?"

"But it's almost noon. You can't lie in bed all day. I spoke to McCall and Maurice this morning. They told me about the fight after the game."

"Okay."

"So...until someone can get ahold of Gus, I need you to be honest with me about everything, okay?"

"You haven't spoken to him?"

"No. He said he'd call or text me when he landed. His flight arrived on time and everything. He even turned off his L.D.S. tail. Do you have Nwaka's phone number?"

"He doesn't have one."

"He did say they'd be hitting the grounds and running. Not sure what he meant, but maybe his phone is dead. I just don't see why he'd take this long to at least tell me something, you know?"

"I think I know."

"Okay? What do you know?" Shauren pleads.

"He probably doesn't want to talk."

"To me?"

"To us."

"Why?"

"That's how it's going to be."

"But is that his way with people?" she asks. "Like with my sister at Thanksgiving? He never apologized for making fun of her weight."

"I'm going to get cereal."

I untuck myself out of bed, and Shauren follows me into the kitchen. Her eyes supervise as I grab a bowl from the cabinet—and judge how I open the 59-ounce carton of almond milk to pour milk into the bowl first. I reach below the kitchen island counter for cereal, and her forehead crinkles. "Cereal's the measure," she says. I grab two handfuls of Golden Trunks, drop them into my bowl of milk, and take a spoon to submerge the cereal. "Why?" she asks.

"Why for what?"

"Milk, and then cereal?"

"Oatmeal burns my throat."

"But you poured the milk first."

"What if I poured my cereal first?" I ask. "Is everything okay with the almond milk?"

"Rigil."

"You say my name like this?"

"Like what?" she asks—but pauses. "Just listen...your frustration, your attitude, it showed on the court yesterday."

"I was protecting myself."

"That won't matter to the people suspending you. You're making me look bad in front of the school board. Fighting players? You could've walked away."

"Which way?"

"To the locker room? Your coaches? I don't know..."

"But I was protecting myself."

"And that's fine, but considering it's the second time you've had an altercation on the court..."

"Okay."

"They'll likely be suspending you for it."

"Okay."

"But are you okay?" she says. "You're going to miss practice."

"Practice?"

"Yes, practice. You can't go to practice until after your LEIP hearing."

"Okay, I won't go to practice."

"So, you're not concerned about LEIP? And what are you going to do instead of practice until Wednesday?"

"Sleep."

"And class?"

"Okay."

"You definitely won't be sleeping here all day."

"But I can after logging off?"

"Why do you want to sleep so much?"

"To protect myself."

"That's not healthy," she says.

"Protecting myself?"

♦
♦
♦

Wednesday afternoon's hearing is held in the Tilikum Conference Room at the end of Joe' Prep's black and red checkered east hall. Before approaching the room, I feel a dodgeball of darts being thrown against the walls of my intestines. It must be the mark of fear, change, or both—by this familiar knot in my stomach. But it's me, not ready for the approaching pull of a shoelace.

McCall paces, walking circles in front of the conference room doors. Two pens are holstered in each of his ears as he praises my arrival. "Great. You look relaxed," he says. He snatches one pen from his right ear and clicks the living ink right out of the ball-pointed end, flooding the east halls of Joe' Prep with a blackened, silky liquid.

The hearing's canceled.

And I... go home.

…we enter the room to three men and a woman sitting at a cherrywood-topped conference table. McCall and I take our seats, and Dr. Brody joins just after, taking command from the big chair at the end of the table.

My chair squeaks three times. But glaring in apparent agitation, a green blazer-wearing gentleman shining his cuff links, coughing and fingering notes into his SpacePad.

"Rigil Ahliko Banks," says Dr. Brody. "How are you this afternoon? You should be well aware of why you're here… and to set the tone for the meeting, I advise you that this session, from here, will be recorded. Anything you do or say can and will be used in the Port Avantian District Court of Law. Has McCall informed you why he's here?"

"Shoot," says McCall. "I was supposed to——."

"Excuse you," Dr. Brody interrupts. "Mr. Rick McCall, Rigil Ahliko must answer."

"Is he a witness?" I ask.

"Rigil, there will be no judgments or decisions made today," she says. "McCall is your acting legal guardian for our proceeding hour. We understand Yusmata, your father, is unreachable at the moment, and Shauren holds a contesting interest."

The gentleman wearing the green blazer raises his finger, "Have you spoken——."

"Mr. Jefferies," Dr. Brody interrupts. "We discussed

order, didn't we? Please hold the questions." She clears her throat and takes a sip out of her green coffee mug. She then eyes McCall, who switches to his left pen that he clicks so fast, so hard, the friction melts the plastic, dissolving the pen onto the wooden tabletop.

"This is Mr. Jefferies," says Dr. Brody. "He's *Gentleman* and our Ambassador representing the Third Commencing Region of Port Avanti's Legislating Sector."

Fine-tuning his face, the familiar jawline my eyes detect. However, his short hair catches me off guard. And I typically do well with smirks.

But not this one.

Shapeshifting in the end chair, he continues shining his cuff links as I'm advised on my potential repercussions for Saturday night's brawl. "Why is Mr. Jefferies here?" I ask.

"Questions will wait," says Dr. Brody.

"...if McCall can't speak either, won't I need a lawyer?"

"That's why I only introduced you to Mr. Jefferies," she says. "McCall is your acting legal guardian until either parental guardian can choose to appoint you one or hire an attorney."

"I don't trust him."

"McCall or Mr. Jefferies?" asks Dr. Brody.

The others at the table who weren't introduced begin noting in their ViDi notepads. As for McCall, his pen gets stuck—he can't click it. He tosses it in the trash and grabs the other from his right ear. This one's stuck as well. So he shoots it toward the garbage like a basketball, but it rims off to the floor.

Mr. Jefferies slowly reaches and presses the recorder's pause button, "Rigil Ahliko," he says. "Is there something you wish to say off-record?"

Dr. Brody also reaches for the recorder, saying, "This is not—"

But Jefferies presses her hand against the table and stops her, "Go ahead," he tells me. "Tokaiya and Yarnell had their time with us. We aren't treating you any different."

"I never understood your purpose."

McCall interrupts, "Can Rigil and I have a moment in the hallway?"

I follow McCall to the hall. His ears are empty, and his hands are free. "Oh boy," he says, checking his pockets. "Got a pen I can borrow?"

"No."

"What's with the attitude?"

"I don't have a pen."

"Okay, that's all you have to say."

"I did…"

"Yeah, and like you wanna stab me with one."

"Okay."

"Okay?" he says. "Just listen. As far as those booj-wah

white folks in there, we spoke, okay?"

"About what?"

"Consequences."

"We did?"

"…are we not clicking here? Am I missing something?"

"Your pen?"

"Rigil…?"

"You say my name like that—"

"It's also how your dad wrote it."

"How do you write it?" I ask.

"Something's missing, remember?"

The first double door cracks open, and Dr. Brody peeks her head out first. "Just one more minute," says McCall. Dr. Brody raises her right palm at us, continuing to swing the door wide open. The note-takers exit first, followed by Jefferies, who turns abruptly into the main east hall. "Everything good?" McCall asks.

Dr. Brody smacks her lips, asking us to return to the conference room table. She insists I take the large chair at the end and advises McCall to shut the door. She clears everything off the table except a box of tissues that she slides toward my hand. "There's never a better time to break such news," says Dr. Brody. "But Shauren's been arrested."

JOURNAL VII
MONDAY—DAY FOUR

THE MIDDLE-AGED WOMAN STANDS in the elevator bank walkway of the 23rd floor, gasping with two large bags in each hand. "How are you this morning, young man?" she asks, dragging her feet across the elevator carpet to the corner. The woman hobbles in a pair of thick-soled grey sneakers as the elevator rocks through its initial descent. She stuffs smaller plastic bags into each pocket of her long green jacket, fluttering her drooping eyes in a longing sigh like an exhausted puppy. She then hunches over, pulling random things out of each linen bag and placing them into the other. "If I could only be young and fit on a Monday morning again," she smiles but stops to look up.

"Want help with your bags when we get to the lobby?" I ask.

She pauses to source my eyes and looks me up and down. "That's nice of you to ask. But I can manage—considering this past weekend was hell."

"I'm sorry to hear that."

"Yeah, well, the entire neighborhood heard it the other night. Where were you then?" she laughs.

"At least you can laugh about whatever it was."

"That's true. But I couldn't tell you how badly I wanted to—" The woman stops to exhale between her bags and looks up at the ceiling mirrors in frustration. "I just hate how they designed these elevators. And poor Chad had so much on his plate, but hopefully, new ownership also does something about the ramp exit out there. I see they're finally working on the courtyard. But have you seen the parking garage exit? It's a death trap."

"I normally come out of the—"

"You must be new to the tower," she says. "Just be careful, okay?"

The best I can do is insist the lady exit the elevator before me.

And so, she does—waddling down the hall, teetering the bags from side to side. Her jacket sways between her steps, acting as a cushion when the bags knock against the sides of her knees. The front lobby doors open, and Deliah enters, holding the doors for the penguin walking lady. They hug in a comforting manner, like a mother seeing her daughter for the first time after months away at college. Deliah helps the woman load her bags into the RyderCar and waves goodbye to her. Deliah reenters the building, striding down the lobby and wiping her eyes as though her heart had fallen into the lady's bags. But she still manages to tighten her red bandana over her forehead and readjust her black sports bra to pull it just below her belly button to cover the first set of her washboard abs. She proceeds to wipe her dusty, moist, sweaty, and toned thighs from a Monday morning gardening session as she approaches. "Poor woman," says Deliah, shuffling work orders on our concierge desk.

"Poor?" I ask. "She lives here."

"Mr. Banks," she says. "Please—"

"It's *Rigel*. Not mister."

"So that's how you say it?"

"My name?"

"Yes," she laughs. "And all this time, I never knew what to call you. I've waited on Perkins to say it."

"He won't say my name. But did he go up?"

"Up?" she asks.

"He's on the 13th."

"This place has a 13th floor?"

"Why do you say it like that?"

"Most buildings don't. It's a thing, ya' know?"

"No," I laugh. "Buildings have a 13th floor. They just call it 14."

"Whatever, but yes, he went up and left these tickets for Wednesday night's symphony."

"For me?"

"For us."

"Together?" I ask.

"No."

"But the seats are together."

"So, you can read?" she smirks.

"…why'd you say *us*?"

"First come, first serve, I assumed."

"I figured. So, they're yours?"

"Let's see…" she ponders, but longer than necessary. "We do have that project in Grossmont this week."

"So, they're mine?"

"You must have someone to take?"

"Sounds like a personal question."

"It's a considerate question."

"We've gotten these from a friend of Chad's since I've been here, and Perkins usually gives them away."

"So it's more of a business option?"

"For who?"

"For you."

"You too."

"How so?" Deliah asks.

"How not?"

"Garden's Pledge is regulated by TheDistrict's Business Commission. Nothing gets written off."

"Sounds like they're mine then."

"But I got to them first."

"And then you said 'us'…"

"In case you have someone to go with."

"And I thought that was personal."

"That's not what I meant," she says.

"But you said what you said."

"Were you listening for a reaction?"

"Doesn't matter, you weren't specific."

"Okay," she exhales. "Then do you want them?"

"Do you have someone to go with?"

"Sounds personal," she winks.

"No. It's business on my part."

"Oh, so I just become your write-off for the evening?" Deliah asks.

"That's assuming I was inviting you to go with me."

"You're taking business to another level now."

"It's still business."

"So, that was an invite?" she asks.

◆

◆

◆

WEDNESDAY—DAY SIX

I meet Deliah at the top step of Jack London Square Station's staircase. She power walks in a long grey trench coat, swinging her pressed hair over her shoulders. The split in her dress slightly exposes her gardener snake thighs peeking through her jacket between succeeding steps. Her natural skin lightens her bewildering eyes. Sharp nose complements her runway jawline. The way she looks at me is nothing less than judgment. She's got me beat. But she wears her status— lurking ahead, hoping it holds.

"Are you hungry or thirsty?" I ask. "The library is three blocks."

Deliah puckers her chin, "I never figured you to be so kind."

"No need to try and figure me out."

"You know what they say—."

"*They* could say a lot of things."

"My mom always told me complex men come off mysterious."

"And a dead clock strikes on time twice a day."

"Excuse you?" she glares.

"That's also what they say… Sorry. Didn't mean to offend you."

"My mother's not a dead clock. She's alive and well."

"Married?" I ask.

"No, she divorced my father."

"Typical."

"Typical?" she says, stopping with a sneering smile across her reddened face. "Do you have a hard time with sympathy or something?"

"No, but I always hear about couples splitting up."

"But your response was rude. And a bit snark."

"Don't take it personal."

"It's just us, Rigil."

"I know. What's the issue?"

Deliah shakes her head. "No wonder you're single. You haven't even apologized."

"Okay...I'm sorry I had to hear that."

VII.2

WEDNESDAY—DAY SIX

We arrive at an opulent entrance flooded by photographers behind flashing lights for the attention pursuers—all positioned for neck-breaking photos. Across from the Amphitheatre's lobby, Deliah's eyes fixate on the attire of everyone standing, posing, eager for the eyes of...

At coat-check, she stands mesmerized—eyes glossing at every woman's sparkling skirt and glittering brooch. These women also emit the fragrance of success, flaunting their glamorous dresses and posh heels. But it's Deliah's gladiator pumps, marking her spot amongst them and walking as if she owns them. The autonomous valet is crowded with a congregation of Phat-Cats and Big-Men of TheDistrict—all waiting to calm the shock of attention and the bullshit agreement of the Avantian hierarchy.

We're ushered to our seats at the first-row balcony mezzanine. Deliah removes her jacket and tosses it over the balcony railing. Her backless lace-up exposes her rising goosebumps but is concealed by the cloth-backed seat. She sits with her legs crossed, shaved smoothly like an infant's buttocks. Her eyes scan the audience at the orchestra level, where the Avantian Symphony sets the stage before them with the saxophonists, brasses, windpipes, strings next to the keyboards, and percussionists at the rear stage. The probing out of her eyes molds her into the vulture she could be—and scold she can mock…

"No."

Deliah's a flower who hasn't seen such elegance. A bird whose wings learned to tap into flight this morning. In her early stages of lift-off, she acclimates to her new views above an old normal. She's also me, trying to remember this is business. And by all means with intended purposes, I don't know how to act in this fancy-ass place either. What I do know, a flower blooms for its first time every spring.

Budding in my imagination, her thoughts, strings of cords such as violins, cellos, and double basses… creating a terminal between our collaborating tapping feet to the timpanists.

The conductor quiets the orchestra. And the crowd waits.

…until a dreadlocked saxophonist stands to his feet, preparing his horn for the business. He blows upwards through his shut-eye solo, swinging the horn between his knees and around his hips.

Beneath him, the orchestra level audience watches beside each other's drooping jaws. Deliah uncrosses her leg, leaning closer to the blow as her hair flings over her left shoulder blade. "He's pretty good," she says, swinging her hair back.

The conductor faces the audience and spreads his arms for everyone to stand. He points at the front row and signals for them to clap. After the applause makes its way to the back row of the orchestra level, Deliah and I stand with the rest of the mezzanine level's front-row audience, clapping in sync, palm to palm. "It sounds so beautiful, don't you agree…" she says. But I step into the aisle, make my way up the mezzanine steps, and watch the balcony level close out their applause. I turn back, and Deliah mouths, "Where are you going?"

.
.
.

Rollin Noodles…because it's the one urban place closest to the Library's Amphitheatre where I can calmly untether the stuck-up nose I had to pucker at the symphony.

Rollin' Noodles…because none of their poultry broth is

heavily infused with thick ocean-deep salt water.

Rollin' Noodles…because the lightly salted chicken won't overstimulate my red blood cells evacuating cortisol hormones after coming down from a heightened sense of… being the person I'm not meant to *breathe*.

"Wow," says Deliah. "I love how they do their noodles."

"They're made in the back."

"Aren't they made from scratch?"

"Yeah, they're rolled in the back."

"Ahh," she says. "Rollin'…how original."

"And it's the only building west of Capitol Parish still using tills."

"What are those?" she ponders.

"The machine up front where they're doing take out."

"I thought those were the first SpacePads.

"It's basically a cash register."

"Umm…"

"Really?" I ask.

"I know of one type of tilling, and it's what pays the bills."

"Of course you do."

"Before you called us, did you see 'till' in my company's name?"

"No. I only read your worst reviews."

"Oh gosh. Those break my heart."

"I mean, if you'd been operating Garden's Pledge through a SpacePad, we wouldn't be here."

"What's a SpacePad got to do with it?"

"They have to manually audit you."

"Are we not supposed to be doing business with you?"

"You're doing business with Tower 521."

"But aren't you an Avantian?" she asks. "And did you not learn the rules of LEIP in high school?"

"…thought you didn't like getting personal?"

Deliah finishes the last of her Sake and keys in another round from our table's SpacePad menu. She continues perusing the screen as the punk rock stair-sitters at our right do so at the mercy of their L.D.S. displays. The line outside the door doubled in capacity since we'd arrived, amplifying more chattering loudmouths and becoming the soundtrack to our symphonic after-party.

"So…have you been here before?" Deliah asks.

"…*trains, mirrors, and nosey white people.*"

"You love making an awkward moment," she says. "I take it this isn't your scene?"

"*Shrugs.*"

"Where are you from, originally?"

"Valleys of TrenchPort."

"Really? It's so nice. My girls are planning a trip there next year. If I can get the time off, I'll join them. Do you ever go back to visit family?"

"No."

"Why not?"

"Elephants are too big to go back for."

"Isn't dumbo an Asian elephant?" she asks.

"Ha, that's debatable."

"Or did they torture him for his ivory?"

"Or so he wouldn't hurt himself."

"Interesting," she says.

"But I'm impressed by your research."

"Thank you," she smiles. "Just connecting the dots. But your family, are any of them back in Africa?"

"Where?"

"Africa."

"Africa?" I ask.

"Yeah," she responds. "Do you have family over there?"

"The people of Tower 521 are my only family."

Deliah laughs so hard that the kid beside us drops half his coiled noodles back into the steaming broth. "You're kidding?" she asks, covering her mouth.

"I've done more for our residents than they'll ever know."

"They don't even know who you are."

"The ones who matter do."

"Perkins doesn't count," she says. "And what about Ms.

Hammock?"

"Who is this?"

"The lady who got into an accident Friday night."

"Doesn't sound like she's on my radar."

"You were just on the elevator with her on Monday," Deliah claims. "Perkins has been ordering her RyderCars all week to Uptown since her car got hit that night. Speaking of, what's up with that garage ramp off of Knolls?"

"I don't know. I exit onto Grant."

.

.

.

Deliah and I approach Jack London Square Station's arching phosphorescent lights as the flickering signs glimmer a color of nodes spiraling against the reflective windows of the hotel's 21st floor. I could close my eyes abruptly and still see the lights dancing across the back of my eyelids with the phosphenes, much like the night fires over yonder I'd watch with *them*. It was a dry evening when we first walked this path to switch from one hotel room to another at the lead of a slick exile turned martyr. Over the years, I've passed here many times through the GTube below—but walk it today, only to reminisce next to an ignorant, ego-driven gardener who'll never understand my days of burning oats and water. She'll never overstand Mahan's path, constructed by eye floaties at the heights that even an elusive Malimbus bird won't fly. She'll never understand how close I once was from delusionally bowing to the symphony from the red-walled rooms across from the Library's Amphitheatre.

"That third window from the left," I point. "That's one of the hotel rooms we first stayed in when we got here."

"Wasn't it a motel?" Deliah asks.

"Yeah, and we set it on fire. Well, I did. By accident."

"Why?"

"My sister made me mad."

"So, you lit it up?"

"It was an accident. I tried to scare her."

"My gosh," she says. "What'd she do or say?"

"I don't remember."

Deliah jumps in front of my step, and my foot smothers her right gladiator toe. "Rigil, look at me," she glares. "Just tell me. I know you have a sharp recollection."

"Why do you care for?" I ask. Her bottom lip sinks, covering the upper part of her chin. "Okay, so my sister said I was special—and compared me to someone."

"And you took it as an insult?"

"Sure."

"Was this person a friend?"

"Was. He didn't make it out of TheValleys."

"I'm sorry to hear that… But did I go too far? Are you okay?"

"Some memories shouldn't—."

"Shouldn't?" she asks.

Deliah hooks her arm around my elbow but is a bit too aggressive as her heel is caught on the edge of the top step. She loses her balance, and her right leg collapses like a single raw noodle—forcing her to grab my forearm to keep from sliding. But then her left heel slips from the second step, sliding her further down the staircase. She clinches my hand tighter, gasping, squealing, as she has no choice but to rest on her back across the top of the steps. I kneel to my feet and pull her up by her armpits, saying, "No need to be embarrassed."

"You probably think I'm drunk."

"No, but I find it hard believing you did gymnastics."

"…that's the best you can say?"

After boarding the train, Deliah goes ear first, resting her head on my shoulder.

"My stop's coming up," I tell her, prodding her head off my lap. "See you in the morning?" I ask.

She flinches awake, stretches her back, and buckles my hand. The train comes to a complete stop, and she takes the lead, pulling me through the doorway at arm's length. I'm led to the top of 66th station's staircase, where we're linked by the arms at ground level. Her legs begin trembling two blocks from Tower 521, leaving me to escort her across the street and, somehow, into the building and up to my apartment.

She's a bit of a sloth, removing her jacket and heels, which have somehow sprinkled glitter all over my apartment—especially across my writing nook's futon where she's made herself comfortable. I sit next to her, and she grapples my pants zipper, whispering gibberish around my nape. "Say yes, just yes," she moans.

My legs…separating by the triceps she edges our courtyard below.

My cheeks…caressed by the palms, planting May's flowers to bloom.

My thighs…she elbows, yet gently enough to salute my soldier to half-mast.

"We both have work in five hours," I whisper.

"You don't work," she says, yanking her back against the futon. She whips her neck against the headrest and faces upward, exposing her sclera whites in stillness. I gently reposition her neck because the last thing I want is for my contractor to start work tomorrow with a crook in her neck.

◆

◆

◆

"Can I use your phone?" I'm awakened by Deliah's fool-bright, wine-stained eyes leaning in my doorway. "I need to tell the guys we're starting late," she begs.

She unplugs my L.D.S. from the kitchen island holster and paces up the steps of my writing nook, conversing with her hands.

…her call ends, but she remains staring through my phone screen. "I'm in your city tonight," she says aloud.

"What's that about?"

She tosses the phone onto my bed. "It's a text from a 'Jessica.' And my guys will be pulling up in ten minutes. What else can go wrong?"

"Okay. You go through my phone—."

"Don't you have a car? Can you drive me home?"

"We'd have to leave now. We have a situation with our service elevator. Remember?"

"Dammit."

"Damn what?" I ask.

"Look at me…"

"Why do you care?"

"Um, hello?"

"No one's gonna remember you from the—"

"You're rude," she says. "I'll get a RyderCar."

"Let's go. I'll text Perkins."

"Do not, tell him I'm with you," she pleads, collecting

her purse and strapping on her heels.

Perkins notifies me that shaft three has been clear for seven minutes. In order to secure it for 32 floors, we'd have to log it for the commission's audit next quarter.

And so, we don't do that.

We enter elevator three, taking a rear corner of our own. Descending 32 levels of pure luck, we're approaching the lobby, and our feet begin pressing against the floor. Deliah inhales her corner of air as the elevator door opens to our lobby walkway. Santos passes behind the entering resident, carrying their duffle of tools through the lobby. Deliah tucks her chin. She side-eyes my corner. And I glare up toward the ceiling mirror, praying into my panther eyes as the whites around my pupils glow through the reflection of light. Deliah inhales as Santos steps out of sight of the elevator door's opening view. But a hunched-over Guala follows, watching the resident's footsteps enter the elevator and step in front of Deliah to push the 'close door' button.

The resident exits at garage level one, and Deliah exhales, asking, "So, who is Jessica?"

VII.3

THE DAYS AT CENTAURI

We meet in the Centaurian territories of Chesapeake, where the first Avantian university campus stretches across the southern borders of Port Avanti. The prominent campus is known for its pyramid libraries and spherical lecture halls painted black and white—also strategically placed between green lawns and rocky paths. From its multi-colored Lego-block-looking engineering halls to the registrar's Taj Mahal, the campus has built enough visual stimuli for us on the spectrum to never feel the anxiety of final exams. Not because the grading scale was removed but because everything always looks extravagant. I usually sneak out after curfew and walk to The Bridge of the Red—where we're reminded, as humans, to find contentment in our dark side without forgetting the goodness we seek every day. The Avantian Board of Understanding got a lot of backlash for allowing this message to be expressed anywhere on campus. Because, at first, ordinary people were told to just shut up about it—no one's being forced to send their kids to South Centauri State to study amongst the extraordinary. But ultimately, they got it.

The freshman athletic meet-and-greet banquet kicks off beneath our full Strawberry MOON two months before students move into campus dormitories. Before approaching *her* at the juice bowl, I study her chubby lips, plum pupils, and iris-polished eyes encircled as bright as our MOON up high. She leans against the red banquet wall, majestically sipping her orange cup of juice and alluring into the juice bowl. I cautiously walk over to the red wall, and she turns her shoulder as though I've fallen out of her peripheral. She looks toward the white wall where my teammates converse, and ignores my presence coming into her space near the juice bowl table. I reach for a cup, and she turns back to the juice bowl to grab the punch bowl ladle for a scoop of juice. She pours, topping off her cup and, "Oops," she says. "Did I get your shoes?"

"Yes."

"Well, I'm sorry. Are there napkins over there?" We both look toward the other end of the table where the protein cookies and mixed fruit bowls are placed.

"…napkins must be on the other side?" I ask.

"Of what?"

"The fruit."

"I don't know," she says. "But hopefully, they have club soda down there." We look down at my leather canvas shoes; they're beige, and the red juice stain soaks the toe area. "Are you going to do something about that?" she asks.

"Put it in my laundry basket for our staff?"

"Football team gets maids?"

"You think I play football?"

"I know you do," she responds. "You're in a photo with Maurice on his gum wall. You guys came from—"

"So, you've seen me?"

"I see you now," she says, sticking out her hand. "But can you get a napkin for your shoes?"

"Yes. I'm named Rigil. And I'd shake your hand, but if you couldn't tell, I gotta wipe the juice."

"Yeah? That's how you were taught to greet women?"

"I would've had a plan, but it's the juice," I respond—but she tickles her eyelids. "What's that mean?"

"I'm from The Burg'. What about you?"

"Where's that?"

"Blotsburg."

"Oh. I know that place."

"I'm aware you should," she says. "I'm Jessica, by the way."

"Hi. I moved here in middle school."

"From where?"

"I wasn't born here."

"I'm aware," she says, counting her fingers. "But you sound like you're from around here."

"How?"

"The way you talk."

"How is that?"

"Avantian," she says. "But that doesn't tell me where you're from."

"I came from The Valleys of Trench Port."

"Africa?"

"But my dad wasn't born there."

"Africa?" she repeats.

"He wasn't born there. But he brought us here."

"In middle school?"

"Yes."

"Why are you so difficult to talk to?" she asks.

Her exit from our conversation proves her soul stands at bay. Or maybe it rushes at the gates of her corneas. But for now, she's my match met in Mahan, standing slim-toned, topped by greasy curly hair hanging past her shoulders.

...neither does she walk like her softball teammates.

One of my teammates prowls toward her with his fresh bowl of fruit as she crosses the banquet's dining area to the west-end corner, where the walls are white and gradient yellow toward the ceiling. Another one of our redshirt sophomores joins them at her right elbow, where they all exchange words within 30 breaths of mine.

...I wonder why it didn't last longer.

I'd reapproach her, but I'm good at watching.

Lone wolves don't play in that circus.

♦
♦
♦

The night before fall term's classes start, my dorm room fridge is aired out after I'd finished my post-practice meal of cubed potatoes and pickled steak strips. And Maurice, hired as South Centauri State's head athletic trainer, put me on a diet to cut 25 pounds of jelly by game one.

I was hungry.

A lot.

So I ate—

…and often when I wasn't supposed to.

Our campus unity center closes at 9 o'clock, so I skip Bridge of the Red and walk down Campus Row, where I notice the open café. I presume a sandwich could be heated up in there because the blue light is on. And the red light is…

An old bell rings on the interior doorknob as I enter. The first pair of eyes the bell grabs are *hers*. I knew something was different about that girl—who stares—daring me to sit across from her opened journal. "So, I mean, hi," I stutter.

"You're bold," she says. "Rigil, right?"

"Jessica?"

"Yes," she responds, sipping her tea.

"Can I sit?"

She glances over her right shoulder and takes another sip of her tea—then glances over her left shoulder but leaves the cup on the table and ponders over the steam, saying, "My boyfriend is in the bathroom." Behind the purchase station, one worker lounges on his SpacePad. To his left, an opening into the kitchen, separated by their waist-high partition. The bathroom mirror 15 feet to the worker's left is wiped clean— reflecting a monster amongst his new devil in a stained dress. "Anyways, how's practice?" she asks.

"Well, I'm here. Famished."

"They feed you guys?"

"...bird seeds."

"When's curfew for y'all?"

"In 15 minutes. What are you doing here?"

"I hate my roommates," she says. "So, I'm writing about that."

I scoot my chair closer to the table, and she raises her forearms to the tabletop, covering her journal. Her resting bitch face suggests my eyes stay off her written words by her plump blueberry pupils warning my curiosity without a word off her sacred tongue. Her body is tense but lightly floats above her chair, just enough to where I don't feel awkward about sitting. I don't feel awkward about staying. I don't feel awkward about her.

"Autism must look different in girls."

"So, what's your deal?" I ask.

"What? My major?"

"You're—."

"Don't tell me I'm different. Are you hungry? Eat something," she suggests.

And so I grab a bagel sandwich.

"We can tack this on my student account," I say as I return to my seat.

"You're trying to pay for my drink?" she asks, scanning

the cafe.

Jessica closes her journal and throws it into her shoulder bag. She slides out of her seat, grabs her tea, and takes three long steps to exit the café. Dead-eyed on the bottom of the plastic chair where she'd sat, I'm alone with my sandwich.

She bangs on the glass window beside me, shouting from outside, "Rigil, let's go." I point toward the pay station. "No," she mouths, pointing toward the doors. She folds her lips and slides her index finger across her throat in a slashing motion. I take a bite of my sandwich, wrap up the rest, and recoil my guts to walk out.

"What was that about? Did you pay for us?"

"Walk faster," she urges, snatching my hand. "Fuck this entire campus."

"They have cameras."

"They also have a church on the west side of campus where I can seek forgiveness again next week."

"If I get—."

"Thanks for coming out," she says. "It means a lot."

.

.

.

Jessica studied functional brain typology at the Blue Sphere lecture hall of Centauri State. She knows the brute force of a monster's Thursday bite—especially after it's been in a pre-launching crouch position, wiggling its butt in anticipation of attacking a clumsy calve. A calve whose mother has been in hiding after the poachers attacked—and fate is at the belief that brown grass has just enough minerals to eventually turn green come spring. Her wisest Native American elder taught her to hang the MOON and color the grass when all shades were darker than the tribe's tallest bison.

He died.

…and just before she learned about her East African ancestry, her Avantian mother told her she'd only explain that side of her family once her father returned.

VII.4

THURSDAY—DAY SEVEN

Perkins buzzes her in and sends her up through elevator four. Before walking through my corridor, temp control powers on, blowing dust mites across my living room rugs. Getting bitten before seeing Jessica is me having a really bad time, before knowing I'm going to have a really bad time.

And so, she knocks, presses on my door's entry pad, and knocks thrice more. I slide open the door, telling her, "It takes one knock."

"But good evening?" she says, scratching her eyelid. "I like what you all did downstairs."

"The lounge was my idea."

"Good. Where we can drink?" she asks, walking beside me through the apartment corridor. She scopes the nook, side-eyes my sky panel, and pushes her luggage to the steps. "What was there before the bar?"

"Pool tables. Perkins has the other one. We moved a lot of stuff after... ya know?"

"What?"

"People."

"Rigil Ahli," Jessica says, pointing to her nose. "This girl no longer keeps up with—."

"They marched all the way from Laurent'co circle."

"What..."

"And set the lawns on fire."

Jessica rolls her eyes. "Oh my gosh, when?"

"I'm not going to talk to you about this anymore because I know you don't care."

"I care about your tower," she says.

"It'll still be there tomorrow..."

"Sad," she says, with a hissing inhale through her nose. Jessica places her luggage across the nook futon, opens it, and discreetly examines my cushions from left to right. She flares her nose to hover over my writing nook's desk and gawks at the courtyard below.

"What's wrong?" I ask.

"You must love the view from here." Jessica continues to lurk, eyeing the gardening crew and loathing the very breath she holds. "I need to be drunk for this," she whispers.

"What are you looking at?"

"Nothing. Let's drink."

Jessica and I arrive at the lobby, where Perkins paces through the walkway with both arms locked behind his back. "You must have something for me?" I ask.

Perkins swings his arms to his waist, holding Deliah's work orders and a pair of red soiled fingerless gloves with stained white tape hanging from their stiff, mucky seams. He sets everything across the concierge desk, spreading them in a dealer's fashion, asking, "Missing a pair of punk rock mittens?"

"Not those," I respond.

"Ms. Woolly found these buried next to our storage shed."

"Lost and found or toss them."

"They have initials," says Perkins. "Maybe they belong to a resident?"

"But they're stained, and no one's been out there for a while."

"They might just need a good wash…"

Jessica picks them up with the tips of her fingers. "Maybe soak them long enough, and someone will want them. Who found these again?" she asks, sniffing the gloves.

"Ms. Woolly," says Perkins.

"Is she new?"

"That's Deliah," Perkins clarifies. "She's the landscaper out there."

Jessica throws the soiled gloves back on the desk, turns her face upside down, and walks away. Perkins grabs the work orders and scans them into our digital drive, singing:

> *"How did I get so far gone…*
> *My mind steered wrong,*
> *I carry regrets and,*
> *Now I walk alone,"*

Jessica sits in our most comfortable lounge chair facing the lobby walkway. She pulls the ottoman closer to her legs, lifts one leg over her knee, and chews the shit out of two wooden toothpicks she found placed beside the armrest.

…both split by the minute our bartender finishes our Bourbons.

"Tell me about *ThePeople*," Jessica says, sipping her drink.

"I was upstairs."

"Scared?"

"No. Safe."

"At least you got a pool table out of it—and interim

owner?"

"Not really."

"But you're signing checks," she says.

"Sort of…"

"Okay?"

"I have constituents."

"Who?"

"People."

"Residents?" she asks.

"No."

"Then who?"

"Bigger men than—"

"You?"

"That's rude."

"Then fuckin' talk," she begs. "…you still working on communicating with women?"

"No. Just you. But I'm selling the building."

"Good. Pack your luggage. Come play on planes with me… Do that too—and think about it."

"Naw. I'm going with the flow."

"You couldn't…" she says.

"Why so?"

"Look at your apartment—and you've never hired a cleaning lady."

"I'm allergic to dust."

"Right…" Jessica mumbles. She then gleams down the lobby walkway and past the elevators, gazing further through the courtyard entrance. "What are they doing out there?" she asks. "Shouldn't Perkins be at his desk?"

"Possibly. Why?"

"Perkins… and that girl?"

"She's our contractor."

"Mmm, kay."

"He's worked this property longer than anyone on staff."

"You're terrible at reading people," she says. "I suggest you keep an eye on her, okay?"

"Or else what?"

"I will."

"How?"

"You'll see," she says. "And finish your drink. Let's leave. I don't like the vibe here."

Jessica chugs her drink and chews an ice cube from the bottom of her cup. Her tongue figure eights the last block of ice as she stares, daring me as I ask, "Want a lollipop?"

"Here she comes," Jessica whispers, watching Deliah carry her duffle of tools and a shoulder bag. She slouches in her chair, grinning, whispering, "She's dressed like she's going to bible study."

"Hey," says Deliah. "Just finished up. And thanks for signing the forms today."

"Working late, huh?" Jessica interrupts.

"Thank you," I tell Deliah. "I'll be down in the morning before you all get started."

Jessica kicks my shin, begging, "Care to introduce us?"

I respond, "I'm sure she's just trying to get home."

"That's okay," Deliah responds. "I'm Deliah—"

"Hi," Jessica smiles. "You need a drink?"

"Oh, no," says Deliah. "I'm exhausted and have a train to catch."

"Aren't you heading to 66th Station?" Jessica asks. "We'll get a drink for you to go." Jessica, again, kicks my leg, urging, "Three Bourbons. Tell him, and now. She has a train to catch, Rigil."

"Please, don't say my name like that."

"Do you think I give a fuck?"

"You know you could leave?"

"Really, bro?" says Jessica, shooing me away. "Just get our drinks. And make 'em strong." Halfway to the bar, I turn around, and Jessica's blowing kisses at me. She grabs Deliah and pulls her toward the lobby entrance, speaking the 'girly girl' in her ear. "Oh my gosh," Jessica praises. "I love your hair. And I'm sorry, is it Delilah or Deliah?"

.
.

Jessica and Deliah board before me and sit next to each

other as temporal friends. I sit across, giving Jessica a clear view to pierce through my eyes and gleam directly out the window behind me. "Did you know birds fly by just tapping their wings?" Jessica claims.

"I think it's more of a muscle reaction," Deliah responds. "It's like when we walk—"

Jessica turns, facing Deliah as they mirror each other's crinkling foreheads. "Oh my gosh," she says. "I can just study you."

"Really? That's nice of you."

"Hey," Jessica shouts, lunging over to kick my leg. "What are you thinking about? Why so quiet?" She turns to Deliah's ear, whispering, "He gets in his head when he's drunk."

"I'm letting you 'study' her."

Deliah laughs, "You two sound like brother and sister. I can't…"

"But you can tonight," Jessica responds.

"Yeah, right," says Deliah. "I've got so much work in the morning. This drink is gonna knock me out."

Jessica gives Deliah and me the look of a girl who never understood her place on the spectrum—including everyone who admired her.

"You're exhausted," says Jessica. "We get it. You two had all the fun without me last night."

"It wasn't all like that," I respond.

"Are you sure, Mr. Ahliko?" Jessica says, fluttering her eyes.

"Is there something between you two?" Deliah asks.

"Nope," Jessica smiles. "We're just two peas in two completely obscure pods, right?"

"You're doing it again," I tell her, shaking my head.

"Doing what, Rigil?"

"Acting like a bitch."

Jessica turns, glares down the train, and finishes her drink.

"That was rude," says Deliah.

"No," Jessica responds. "Come with me. Let me tell you what he did to me in college."

Jessica grabs Deliah's hand, pulls her up from her seat, and walks her toward the other end of the train. Halfway down, Jessica turns around and shares the length of her middle finger with me as they pass the bending point of the GTube car. Jessica swings her hair to the backside of the carbon fiber paneled seats to face me and shouts, "It's the last train to Saint Laurent'co Circle."

But is it me? Am I the only one on this train who hears her?

"Oh my gosh," Jessica shouts. "Last night must've been lavish!"

As we arrive at SouthStation, Jessica's painted the front

of the train red as her eyes blacken the underground MOON like a jaguar in its sniper position, preparing to pounce on her prey.

The train stops.

Deliah gets off first and immediately heads for track one. She rushes past the dreadlocked saxophonist, assembling his horn. Jessica staggers off next, dragging her feet across the ground. "What'd you put in her drink?" Deliah asks, chuckling down the platform. Jessica gathers herself, holding her cup up high while stepping into a firm, upright walk. She crumples her cup and tosses it at a trashcan near three kids rolling up, but it rims off to the side and onto a white tile of the checkered platform. "Hmm, dust yourself off and try again," Deliah smirks.

Jessica turns back, picks up the cup, and places it into the trashcan. Meanwhile, Deliah and I hurry across track one as the cross gate comes down. "Maybe I'll see her on the other side?" Deliah says, waving goodbye to Jessica. But Jessica sprints down the platform and crouches beneath the cross gate just in time. As we pass a mother wrapping up her baby, Deliah looks over her left shoulder for her approaching train while Jessica speedwalks within arm's length of us. Jessica extends her arms to pry herself between us and aggressively steps ahead—causing Deliah to trip over her right foot—and her left leg to fold like woolly yarn. Deliah collapses off the platform with her arms flailing recklessly over the most gritty tile of the ground.

The baby cries. She hollers. And the mom straightens her breast as this tempered shouting baby tugs her mother's brown and beige blanket. Three kids smoking boogers…they light up behind the shadows of SouthStation's track three neon-green flickering signs. At the end of track four's platform, a couple, both wearing earbuds, steadily peruse their phone.

They see nothing.

The panhandling transient near the staircase pulls back his dreadlocks and ties his hair behind his neck. He picks up his saxophone, closes his eyes, and blows so gently that the baby hushes and ever so gently. The mom turns, stands, and rocks her baby toward the woodwind-playing dream blower.

He hears himself.

Subtle and meek—yet aggressive with his fingers piping the horn's echo down the empty tunnel, the walls catch his five-note rotation—a resonance absorbed through several ear canals, oblivious to two dummies, of which one who can only say…

The studious lady sitting at one end of the L.D.S. charging station ear hustles the conversation between the security guard and a frequent rider at the other end against the wall. The glistening black and white checkered platform reflects her face, inhaling its newly shined surface buffered after rush hour. She feeds the birds breadcrumbs picked out of her paper bag. I can't tell what kind of bread, but there's enough for the entire flock. A gentle lady, to say the least. Frantic, however, switching between her notebook and typing manically on her recharging phone.

.
.

 The train pulls off on track one further down the blue and orange illuminated tunnel as Jessica stands with her jaw dropped low enough to graze the most glistened black tile of the platform. Jessica's bent forward, her jacket hanging halfway off her shoulders, and her hands smothering her mouth to where you'd think she lost a tooth. She's flung her coiled hair over her forehead, covering half her face and watering eyes. "I barely touched her," Jessica whispers.

 "Relax," I respond.

 "Does she have vertigo?"

 "Shhh, no one's looking."

 "Is she epileptic?" Jessica asks, scanning the platform and peeking down at track one. "She's still there."

 "Doing what?"

 "What do you think?"

"I don't know. It's why I asked."

"Look for yourself."

"Don't be suspicious."

"Then shut up and do something," she says.

"The entrapment must've caught her. Hopefully, it's just a body shock."

Jessica glances around the station, yanking my arm. "Let's go," she urges.

"What? There are cameras."

"Fuck those cameras."

"Listen to you."

"Look at you...You have no idea what to do."

"Neither do you."

"I said let's go."

"Where?" I ask.

"Hell, for now... We look suspicious standing here."

"Okay—relax...Let's go with the flow and do the right thing."

"Dead fish go with the flow," she says. "Let's go."

"We can't just leave her."

"I can..."

"Where are you going?"

Deliah lies curled beneath the platform as the train pulls off further beside the strip of blue and orange lights fading down the tunnel. Jessica makes her way past the dreadlocked saxophonist, walking higher up the steps to where I can't see her feet.

It seems the baby fell asleep but maybe yoked off secondhand smoke, fired up by the punks lighting numbers near the trash. Their train approaches on track two, and they board along with the student who tosses her last pile of breadcrumbs at the birds. "Excuse me, mam," shouts the security guard, running to the train as the door signal flashes. He holds up high an L.D.S. charger block for the student to see.

"Oh my," says the student. "Thank you so much." The door reopens after shutting halfway, and she grabs her L.D.S. charger block from the security guard. The student unzips her backpack, and two notebooks slide out. Folders and papers fall across the yellow 'Mind the Gap,' but the security guard helps by holding the door.

I jump from the platform's ledge, swinging below and landing in the fail-safe compartment beneath. It's been 25 years since knowing how it feels to see that it's just a body at this point. Two and a half decades since feeling the aura of airflow around a soul in exodus—a bare sensation in reaction to a vessel being emptied and flatlined next to old soda bottles, hamburger wrappers, and trash blown along brightened train tracks.

I could leave. Jessica and I could go someplace and start

new. But I've jumped. And here I kneel—checking for a pulse I know isn't there. I wonder what's next for Jessica. What's next for me? So be it; this is my flow, I have no paddle, and my rudder's gone rogue—steering me through the white waters of repressed rage and jealousy.

And so, do I sail alone?

Drifting in solitude,

Yet sourcing the choices.

To be a good boy—yeah?

"Have I ever?"

["Shrugs."]

…neither has she.

.

.

"Let me see your middle finger," I ask. "Now tap it against the bottom of your chest."

I grab Jessica's finger as her tear drips onto my knuckle. "My sternum," she says.

"Press here. Feel hollow?"

"Okay, whatever." My middle finger bounces off her echoing chest, and she follows, thumping, mimicking a drumbeat to her breath. "Am I supposed to—."

"Shhh," I tell her.

At the 30th tap, Jessica's head falls back and turns as level-three's GTube air vent blows the tarp away from

Deliah's right hand. "Ahli, I can't——."

"Just keep tapping and breathing with me, please?" I tuck the tarp tighter around Deliah's shoulder and arm, and the 3:00 a.m. sewage flush begins flowing. "You smell that?"

"Gross," says Jessica.

What appears to be dripping snot from the ceiling, falls with a rush of sewage water being sucked from the connecting canal pipes. The airflow suction pulls waste from off the walls, as particles and things without a name come flying off like post-it notes. What reeks of spoiled milk and week-old baby diapers is now at the foot of our fate and the head of our destiny because sometimes, it's not about making the right decision, but making the decision, right.

"All this flows out to the marine outfall until later morning."

"Is there enough water to carry her through the pipes?" Jessica asks.

"It'll fill up; just wait. TheDistrict's sewage is designed after pipe systems beneath TrenchPort...they're flushed every night."

"What if——."

"Keep talking and thinking like that, and someone will. I took care of——"

"Took care of what?" she asks.

"We just gotta be sure *she* floats further down this canal.

We'll climb back up in a few hours."

"Hours?"

"Keep tapping. Right here."

"Have you done this before? ...feel like you've gone sociopath on me."

"No, not this time."

But I might have... finding relief in watching the heavier water flow fill the canal—and more waste gather around the tarp to flow further with it.

Jessica, again, wipes four teardrops off her cheek, covering her nose and hiding her disenfranchised face to plead, "Explain where we go from here."

"Now it's a *we* thing?"

"The fuck is that supposed to mean?"

"One thing at a time, okay?"

"I left to avoid this," she says.

"Or because you're a coward?"

She pounces off the grimy wall, swinging wide at my face. I palm her right fist, and her left hammers against my bicep, attacking like a stray mountain cat. "You did this," she screams. "This is your fucking fault. Shit like this has been happening with us since Chesapeake."

I wrap my arms around her elbows as she squirms to let loose. "Can you stop?" I beg, pushing her away. "Give me your phone. I need a light."

"Why? What are you looking at?"

I point her L.D.S. flashlight down the sewage canal, lighting up a bend of water flow. "I think the tarp is hinged on something down there."

Jessica gasps. She smacks her forehead. And smacks her lips. "I really let you talk me into coming back down here for her."

"…you left, and I'm the psychopath?"

Jessica smiles and chuckles, tilting her head back. "You really liked that girl, didn't you? And what makes your life so special that you felt the need to check on her?"

"She's been working at my Tower for a week."

"It won't even be yours in a month."

"But it's where I live, right now."

"…and turned into that man's pet," she whispers aloud. "Just taking things as they come—going with the flow…"

"You should be thanking me. I could've—"

"But you didn't, didn't you?"

"You left me no choice."

"Oops," she smiles.